CW00865128

ISBN 978-0-483-90539-9
PIBN 10501172

For support please visit www.forgottenbooks.com

FREDERICK HAZZLEDEN

A Novel

BY

HUGH WESTBURY

IN THREE VOLUMES

VOL. I

London

MACMILLAN AND CO.

AND NEW YORK

Printed by R. & R. CLARK, *Edinburgh.*

TO THE FRIEND WHO TAUGHT ME

WHOSE COMPANIONSHIP

HAS BEEN MY PRIVILEGE AND ADVANTAGE,

This Book

IS AFFECTIONATELY DEDICATED.

THIS to a friendship which the years increased,
   To it, and out of it ; for well I know,
   If aught of craft and worth these pages show,
That it is yours as much as mine at least.
I am as one who long outstays a feast,
   His guests have gone, the flickering lights burn low,
   Upon his board the gold and crystal glow,
But laughter all is hushed, and song has ceased.
Now through the window of the silent room,
   Across the vacant chairs, steals, cold and gray,
   The tearful breaking of an autumn day,
And evening brightness dies in morning gloom.
The banquet-board is cheerless as a tomb,
   The dust remains, the soul has fled away.

II

We two, long time, together sailed the seas,
   I at the helm, and you, with hand on chart,
   Laying our course, perfect in seaman's art,
To clear each rock, to catch each passing breeze.
To be your comrade, what could better please ?
   Each striving hand to hand, and heart to heart,
   Lightening the labour of the other's part,—
Who tempts the ocean bids good-bye to ease.
Now I alone must shape my course untried,
   And all the past is but a memory fair ;
The good I learned of you, my only guide,
   My sails of hope, my harbour from despair.
If so I float to port upon this tide,
   Thanks to your skill, thanks to your friendly care.

HUGH WESTBURY.

February 1887.

CHAPTER I

"Do you believe in it, Fred?"

"Do you believe in it, Kate?"

An impatient pucker gathered between Kate's black brows as she stepped round the tennis net, vainly endeavouring the while to shade her eyes from the setting sun with her racquet. Kate was evidently lost in contemplation, or she would have discovered that the crossed strings of a tennis racquet make a very ineffectual sunshade. Her opponent was throwing all the energies of his mental and physical nature into the work of keeping three balls in the air together, and, in the distraction caused by Kate's question and his interrogative reply, had allowed one of the balls to drop.

"Why do you treat me like a child, Fred? If a man asked your opinion about anything you wouldn't go on throwing those balls about and thinking of nothing in the world."

The young man dropped the balls at once, thrust his hands into his pockets, and whistled softly.

"My dear Kate," he said, "don't consume me with those blazing eyes of yours; believe me, I'm ready to investigate the miracles of your friend, Mr. Arnitte, by the strictest scientific methods." Then, seeing the girl was really annoyed, he added, "But, seriously, what do you think about them yourself?"

"I think—well, that I don't know what to think."

"A very proper attitude of mind in which to begin an inquiry into the supernatural," he answered with assumed gravity. "If every one exercised your wise caution, Kate, half the impostors who fleece mankind would find their occupation gone."

"Oh! but I don't say that Mr. Arnitte is an impostor."

"Certainly not; blind scepticism is even worse than blind credulity."

Fred slung his flannel jacket across his shoulder, and added, "Shall we walk down to the bay to look at the *Sylph*? You can tell me all about it on the way, you know."

The dark little face, with its half-thoughtful, half-angry expression, brightened at once.

"Oh yes, Fred. We'll go by the 'Apple Walk';" and, evidently pleased to act as cicerone, Kate took her cousin's arm and led him across the lawn.

Before them lay an undulating stretch of cornfields, covering the sides of the ravine, at the head of which stood Lorton House. The wooded grounds of the house, running along the bottom to the beach, divided the fields like a river. From the lawn, down an irregular descent of a mile, you looked over a meandering stream of dark foliage winding its way to the shore through the lighter tints of the cornfields, which lost themselves in the sky line at the top of the slopes on either side of the ravine. Beyond, to the west, were the crooked channels and sandy reaches of Lorton Bay, sparkling and glowing beneath the gorgeous rays of a summer sunset. Lorton Bay was famous for its sunsets, and this evening there was an unusually fine one.

The sun was yet several degrees above the horizon, but had sunk behind a narrow band of cloud which floated in the west. Below it was an amber lake fading away in infinite distance into tender tones of emerald green,— a glimpse of the regions of the blessed, beyond the sea, beyond the falling curtain of cloud, beyond the sun itself, a realm of peace, of grace, of glory, revealed for a few moments to human gaze. Above the cloud-band lay another spectacle. The upper edge had been tossed into a vast chaos, as if by the forces of the passing sun. They had rent a mountain chain, leaving behind ghastly chasms and precipices, and piled-up confusion of rock and ice. Over the scene was a lurid crimson glow, and behind all shot up great beams of golden light, crown-shaped, as though nature was stamping upon her handiwork the symbol of her strength and sovereignty. The clear heavens above were of deepest blue, to north and south played changing tints of purple, and in the east a low line of hills faded in darkening tones of gray into the evening sky.

Kate and Fred stood watching the glorious picture. Presently, like children, laughing "that their eyes were dazzled," they began their pleasant stroll to the shore. At the bottom of the lawn was the "Apple Walk," a narrow path completely enclosed by an arch of ancient apple trees, which the patient hand of some dead and gone gardener had trained when Kate's great-grandfather lived in Lorton House. The "Apple Walk" wound down to the bottom of the ravine, and ended in a mightier arch of elms, called in local speech a "dingle." A low promontory of red sand-stone jutted out from the "dingle" on to the shore, and at the seaward end of it was a rustic seat.

"So your magician read the inmost thoughts of your soul," remarked Fred, as his cousin ensconced herself in a corner of the wooden seat, and the speaker found a place at her feet, and began to toss fragments of stone over the end of the little promontory.

"I don't know what you call my inmost soul; but he told me to think very much of some one, and then he took my hand and looked into my face for an instant, and whispered to me the right name. How could he have told by mere guesswork, out of all the world, the one person of whom I was thinking?"

Fred turned his head sharply and threw a keen glance at the girl, but her features expressed nothing but quiet puzzledom. He

failed to trace the faintest sign of self-consciousness, and muttering, "Very remarkable
indeed," returned to his stone-throwing occupation.

"Of course, you asked him to perform the
same wonder for me?" he carelessly inquired.

"Oh yes. We were talking of your visit
over dinner, and after he had discussed his
wonders for half an hour, mamma told him
that he must convince you first, for we poor
women were under your very severe guar-
dianship, even in the matter of metaphysics."

This time Fred fancied he detected a
twinkle of malice under the simple demeanour
which this black-eyed young woman of three
and twenty had chosen to assume.

*   *   *   *

Fred's mother and Mrs. Wynnston were
sisters. When Fred Hazzleden was only five

years old he lost his mother, and then Mrs. Wynnston, already a widow, had gone with her only child to keep house for her brother-in-law. Fred and Kate were inseparable playmates. The girl, three years younger than himself, ruled him with a rod of iron. It wasn't that the boy was particularly chivalrous or romantically attached to the little gipsy. But he was constitutionally indolent and fond of peace, and hardly had he been promoted from petticoats when a will, inflexible as fate, entered into his life. Mrs. Wynnston used to say that when Kate was in the cradle she invariably had her own way. Certainly she was not unfeminine nor unamiable. No one knew better how to be winning and lovable. To look at her you would have said she was a Spaniard with her black eyes, her masses of dusky brown hair, her dark complexion, through which you could see a strong tide ebbing and flowing with every impulse which moved her. But with all the quick passion of the South she united the steady determination of Northern temperament. She was a queer mixture of characteristics. Her smile was irresistibly sweet, and her frown, puckering her brow over eyes which reddened with passion, absolutely repulsive. She was brave to a degree, helpful to all whom she liked, a bright, interesting little personality in the house, and yet withal a cause of perpetual frictions and anxieties. Every one loved her, and every one wondered how anybody could love such a reckless, masterful child.

The escapades of her childhood had been innumerable, and Fred remembered some of them with rueful amusement. She inveigled him into a hundred juvenile scrapes, and always left him to bear the brunt of them. Once her constant disobedience of her unfortunate governess came to a serious crisis. She did something which she ought not to have done, or left undone something she ought to have done, and committed one of the unpardonable offences of school life. The long-suffering governess presented a formal ultimatum to the too indulgent mother, and Kate, persistently recalcitrant, was sentenced to twenty-four hours' solitary confinement in her room. Fred, passing beneath her window, saw her beckon, and ignored the signal. But he did not go away. He felt no sympathy with the stubborn child, for he knew that she deserved her punishment. He wanted to go and play cricket, yet lingered disconsolately about the prison window. Then he heard the sash raised, and a soft but imperious voice call, "Come up here."

Fred knew that he was lost. With his soul full of resentment against the little tyrant he climbed up the roof of a low outhouse beneath the window, and in a moment two soft young arms were round his neck, and the curly black head of the sobbing child was nestling for comfort on his shoulder. Fred was not a hard-hearted lad, but he wanted to go and play cricket, and besides, had a strong and active sense of humour. So he said, in tones of not un-kindly remonstrance, "But you know, Kitty, you ought to have said you were sorry." Whatever Kate should have been, Fred was sorry at once.

This strange little creature, called to the remembrance of her fancied grievances, dried her eyes, and commanded, "Help me out."

Fred had not bargained for this adventure, but he was accustomed to give way, not so much from weakness of character as from a strain of philosophy in his disposition which led him to imagine that to swim against the stream was a waste of energy when one could float comfortably along with it. He was as active as a goat, and what Kate lacked in physical strength and nerve she made up in strong determination. She was, in spite of her fixed will, a genuine little woman, with a host of feminine weaknesses. She would cry out if a frog jumped up at her feet, and would run away from the mildest-looking mouse that ever peeped timidly from the dark recesses of a hearth. Yet, if any one had induced her to promise such a thing, or had disputed her courage to do it, she would have walked across the paddock where her uncle's black bull Rover reigned solitary monarch of all he surveyed, and where the bravest man in the village would not enter without a pitchfork in his hand.

"Help me out," again came the quiet words of command.

Fred at once held out his hands, and in an instant the child, lithe and cool-headed as himself, was sliding down the slanting slates. To clamber down an old wooden spout was a trifling feat for the boy; for Kate it was a more formidable adventure.

"Help me," again she said, and Fred, by the aid of an old tub, contrived to land her on the ground, all grazed at elbows and knees, and with torn and trembling hands.

"What are you going to do?" he asked.

"We'll go away and be married, and never come back any more, Freddy," was the composed reply.

For once Fred rebelled. He did not want to go away and never come back again; he wanted to go and play cricket, and had a strong conviction that the situation was ridiculous. As to getting married he had a still stronger objection; and the very idea brought to his mind the little golden head and sunny smile of Mary O'Connor, a juvenile playmate of Kate, for whom he nourished, in the secret recesses of his heart, a consuming passion.

"Oh, we can't go away, Kitty," he protested. "I couldn't leave 'Nipper,' you know, and besides, we've no money."

Kate's answer was practical. "Nipper," the companion of Fred's boyish frolics, was asleep in his kennel close by.

The child ran, caught up the dog, and brought him to Fred's feet. "We'll take poor 'Nipper' with us, and I've ever so much money, and you shall have it all;" and she poured into her cousin's reluctant hands a pocketful of hoarded coppers, interspersed with odd sixpences and shillings, the rewards of Kate's very few good and obedient days.

Fred groaned in spirit. He was twelve years of age, and old for his years. He thoroughly realised the absurdity and inconvenience of two small children, accompanied by one cross-bred dog, and furnished with three shillings and elevenpence, chiefly in coppers, going away to get married. Kate, serenely untroubled by any such considerations, was already leading him by the hand out of the yard gate, for they were at the back of the house, and without more ado the pair sauntered down the lane towards the village. Fred was not cheerful. He was dolefully speculating on the result of the cricket match, and at the same time wondering what in the world would become of his obstinate companion and himself when it grew dark. Kate, for her part, was revelling in the bright sunshine, and thinking how much nicer it was to be in a pretty country lane on a hot summer afternoon than to be shut up in one's bedroom.

Still holding Fred's hand she danced along with a kind of shy dignity, noticeable in all her movements. Her mother had taught her some little French ditty, in which *ma mie* was asserted to be everything, both in *ma mort* and also in *ma vie.* This Kate, in her tuneful voice, was humming to herself as the pair approached the long village street. Fred already had become an observer of human nature, and one result of his observation was the conviction that sugar is an infallible solvent of feminine determination. He popped into a little shop, the four-feet-square window of which was employed to display a miscellaneous stock, varying from finnan haddocks to petroleum, and from lucifer matches to sugar - candy. Drawing upon his store of coppers, he furnished himself with a packet of " acid drops," a packet of " London mixtures," and a stick of chocolate. He was tolerably sure now that they would get home again before very late. On the children strolled, not knowing whither. Now in the open fields, where the warm breeze danced across the corn and frolicked round the whispering branches of the trees. Now between shady fern-grown banks, where their feet splashed in the boggy soil, and where ancient, wicked-looking frogs popped their heads out from beneath tufts of marsh grass and tangles of reeds, and, sitting upon their haunches, surveyed with an odious leer the little girl who was running away to be married. But presently the sight of Fred, and the intuitive consciousness which frogs have when boys are good shots with a catapult, sent them quaintly grunting into the recesses of the dyke.

Again, the children's aimless path led them into a fair highway, arched with chestnut trees, between the broad leaves of which the sun's rays glanced and sparkled, casting upon the white road and the rich strips of green turf which skirted it a shimmering fretwork of golden light. The laughter of the children resounded along the deep arches of foliage.

" Burrs," as the natives called them, fallen
from the trees, strewed the ground, affording
a somewhat light but convenient missile to
restless boys, who find tempting marks for a
shot in all kinds of terrestrial objects, from
tomtits to haystacks.   Fred made many an
earnest essay to do execution among the
hedge-sparrows and linnets which, twittering
their tails in the most provokingly imperti-
nent manner in the world, hopped on in front
of them, apparently little disconcerted by the
hail of " burrs " which fell around them.
Fred would have rejoiced hugely to hit a
sparrow, not that he bore the birds any ill-
will, or was inspired by any murderous im-
pulses.   But Kate was at his side; and if
anything ever tended to make a boy try to
aim straight, Kate's black eyes and rare smile
did.   He pictured to himself her unspoken

delight at his prowess and her spoken remonstrance, "Cruel boy!" and with renewed
energy devoted himself to the utterly im-
possible task of slaughtering a bird with a
chestnut "burr."

At last the road, after a sharp descent,
brought them to a spot some three miles
from the village, famous through the whole
midland district. The "Hanging Rocks"
were the northernmost spurs of a chain of bold
hills, running diagonally across the country.
A bridle-path, well known to Fred, turned
from the highway, and led for ten minutes
up a steep climb through a wood of larch and
birches. Then suddenly one of the most
glorious panoramas in all England burst into
view. The "Hanging Rocks" were half a
dozen tremendous heaps of granite boulders
shot up, as it were, through the verdant slope,

and towering, gray and bare, in fantastic confusion, above the tops of the wood. Behind
the stone heaps the path zigzagged twice or
thrice, then came a final scramble over a big
smooth block, and you found yourself stand-
ing on the summit of the "Hanging Rocks,"
looking out over the undulating vista of the
shires. Just below, like a gem, in a rich
setting of foliage, was a tiny lake, on the
banks of which stood a quaint old manor
house, where in the days of Elizabeth a
famous poet had made his home, and where
the bearers of his name still live. Away
beyond, a running glint of gold, interwoven
into the scene, as patient Eastern potters lead
a glistening thread through the strange
medley of their decorative work, showed
where a river ran. In the cornfields the
greens had lost their brightness under the

summer sun, and a painter would have looked for his "Naples yellow" to reproduce some of the distant tones. Far off for thirty miles, to right, to left, and in front, the rolling panorama spread: farmsteads and baronial halls, pheasant woods and noble park timber, patches of moorland, vast stretches of cornland, broken by the dark line of hedges; white thirsty roads, winding away to the vanishing point; and over all, like a blessing of God, lay the mellow glow of evening, and up through the stillness, with a whisper of peace, came the gentle breeze and a distant music of the singing of birds.

Kate and Fred ensconced themselves in the shade of a big block at the very top of the "Hanging Rocks," she seated in a comfortable nook, he sprawling at her feet. Children as they were, each in a different way was susceptible to the influences of lovely scenery. The lad, on such a day and in such a landscape, would experience a sense of almost sadness which, without understanding it, he enjoyed. There was a strain of poetry—sentimentality, if you will—in Fred's nature, thinly disguised by his youthful insouciant philosophy. Throughout his life a very bright day always made him pensive, and a beautiful landscape filled him with vague dreams, in which he delighted more than in the natural beauties themselves.

Kate, on the other hand, had a very keen sense of colour. A bright flower or bird would cause her to cry out with a strange sort of physical pleasure. Intellectual delight in a lovely landscape she had none, but she would sit with dilated eyes drinking in draughts of rich colour, and experiencing much the same sort of satisfaction that a gourmand feels in a very choice dinner.

Now both were looking out over the rich midland country, and enjoying the scene in their different fashions. But Fred was unusually preoccupied. Mingled with his day-dreams was the pressing practical consideration where they were to go next.

He was the first to speak. " Have an acid drop, Kitty," he said. Kate plunged her brown fingers into the packet and extracted a couple. Anxiously Fred watched her consume them, as happy and unconcerned as " Nipper," who lay close by sound asleep in the sunshine. He groaned very quietly to himself and then said, " Have another." Kate took two more. Fred helped himself, and munched and meditated on the situation.

Presently, when the sugar-plums had had

time to exercise their soothing influence,
Fred inquired, " Where are we going when
it gets dark ? "

" I don't know," was the tranquil reply.

" Then we'll go home again. It will be
late before we get there, and aunt will be so
glad to see you again that she won't say
anything about what you did this morning."
The bait took.

Kate pondered awhile, and then returned,
" Mother said I was a bad, obstinate girl.
Will she be glad to see me back ? "

" Oh yes," returned Fred, " she'll be glad,
and I'll be very glad to take you back, and
' Nipper' wants to go too," he added, as the
dog frolicked backwards and forwards about
the rocks, calling his master with perky little
barks.

" Then you don't want to go away and be

married?" The clouds gathered upon Kate's features as she spoke.

Fred laughed a bright laugh and said, "Silly girl! people can't get married till they're grown up. When we are perhaps we shall get married."

One of those vibrations of tenderness which sometimes made her influence irresistible stirred Kate's nature. "Freddy," she said, leaning forward, her voice low and earnest, "Mamma was crying the other day, and I asked her what for. She told me because she had found an old letter from papa. But I didn't know what made her cry; and she said that years ago, when I was a baby, papa died, and now she had no one to help her and be good to her, and that made her sorry. She said papa was very strong and brave, and wouldn't let anything hurt her or trouble her; that he loved her and made her life happy. Freddy, I'm not very happy, and I want some one to love me, and to be brave and help me when I get into trouble, and there's nobody so good to me as you, dear, and that's why I wanted you to come away and get married." The child's voice ended in a sob, and her head drooped in a burst of tears.

Fred's eyes were moistened, and, getting up, he kissed her and soothed her with awkward boyish caresses, vowing to her that he would love her all his life and marry her whenever she liked. Kate was docile enough now, and the pair walked home hand-in-hand to find a state of domestic confusion which Fred had shrewdly foreseen. Mrs. Wynnston had gone into hysterics when Kate's disappearance was discovered and the fall of

evening brought no sign of the fugitives.
The incidents of their return were no surprise to Fred. Mrs. Wynnston seized her
daughter with foolish delight and over-
whelmed her with kisses and reproaches, all
of which demonstrations Kate bore with
perfect equanimity. Fred's father, on the
other hand, spluttering with hasty temper,
ordered him off to bed without any supper,
and threatened certain unpleasant conse-
quences if he appeared again at the family
table for a week. Fred knew that protest
was useless, so he picked up "Nipper," who
was slinking at his heels, and made for the
door. But, just as he was going out, Kate
jumped from her mother's lap, scattering the
sweetmeats and cakes which had been produced for her delectation, and, flinging her
arms round Fred's neck, kissed him and said,

"Never mind, I love you and will make it up to you, Freddy." Fred did mind, though, and when he reached his room employed himself for an hour before going to sleep in feeding "Nipper" with scraps of biscuit, and meditating on the injustice of the world to boys who never did the world any harm and only wanted to be left alone.

* * * *

The majority of men do not perceive the connection between morals and physiography. They wonder why B is so good and his twin brother A so bad, and never take the trouble to notice that A's house is in a valley and faces the south, while B lives on the top of a hill and his windows look north. Let them change residences, and in twelve months A will become the esteemed churchwarden of his parish, a bright brand snatched from the burning, while all the family will deplore B's inexplicable falling away from grace. Depend upon it, the atmosphere has more to do with the conduct of mankind than philosophers and theologians are willing to confess. Why, for example, is St. John's Wood St. John's Wood, and why is Stoke Newington not St. John's Wood. Go to live in the former district, and if you are a thoughtful man you will soon detect a curious relaxing of your moral fibre. Perhaps you have observed all the commandments from your youth up, and have felt no spiritual pride in the knowledge of the fact. Now you will begin to play havoc with the Decalogue. Probably you will break the last commandment first—most men commence at the end and work backwards. So far you have done nothing more than covet your neighbour's house or your

neighbour's wife, and you will feel quite
virtuous because you have not infringed the
other two injunctions relating to your neighbour's belongings.   Not only do you slide
easily along the ways of vice, but you unconsciously adopt a very paltry standard of
virtue.   In Stoke Newington you would
have been horrified if you had broken one of
the commandments; now in St. John's Wood
you regard yourself as a most estimable person because you have not broken them all.
These two districts serve as illustrations of
the atmospheric theory of ethics, but any one
may discover similar phenomena elsewhere.
The atmosphere of Paris, for instance, is
lowering to the moral system.   One has
heard of dissenting deacons taking a holiday
in the French capital.   The first few days
are spent in the Louvre, Notre Dame, and

the Jardin des Plantes. But before a week has passed away these good men, who have always spoken of the theatre as one of the widest gates of Satan's kingdom, are found surveying the ballet at the Opera House; and at the end of a fortnight have seen without blushing the *can-can* at one of the gardens of delight in the Champs Élysée. What another week of Paris air might bring about one shudders to contemplate.

There must have been some influence dangerous to sentimental young men in the warm breeze which diffused itself, rather than blew, across Lorton Bay this evening. The waters of the rising tide plashed with a soothing music against the foot of the sandstone promontory. A quarter of a mile away the *Sylph* rode at anchor, motionless in the calm summer sea. So great was the stillness that the monotonous, soliloquising whistle of the man on deck, who was Fred's captain, mate, and crew, the silent cousins could distinctly hear.

The light faded into that deep gray tone in which a plain woman looks beautiful, and in which a beautiful woman becomes irresistible. Kate was communing with herself, and Fred, who had lighted his pipe, was flinging stones into the water. Two or three times he glanced up in her face, and finally, with a big sigh, got up, knocked the ashes out of his pipe, and seated himself by her side.

"Kitty," he said, with a laugh in which there was a suggestion of embarrassment, "do you remember when we ran away to get married?"

Kate started a little, and in the dusk he

saw the colour deepen on her cheek. "Oh yes," she replied, "I can remember many foolish things we did when children. But shall we not go in ? it is a little chilly."

Fred took her hand in his and continued : "You told me, Kate, then—I recollect as if it was but yesterday—that you were not very happy, and needed some one to be good to you and help you, and that no one was to you what I was. I was a child then, and didn't fully understand what that meant, nor did you in saying it. But I do now. If, dear, you still feel that want in your life, will you let me try to fulfil it ? I've no great talents, or station, or wealth to offer you ; but I can give you a strong and faithful love, and I can try to make you as happy as you will make me if you will become my wife. I've always loved you, dear, without knowing it. Now I know all. Do you love me, lassie?"

He believed it thoroughly. His voice trembled, his hand pressed hers convulsively, his eyes glistened. But it was pure delusion. Until half an hour ago he had never dreamed of marrying Kate Wynnston, and had any one suggested it to him would have been amazed and even irritated. But there was love in the air. His heart was full of pleasant recollections of boyhood, and in a moment he had come to the conclusion that his sincere affection for his cousin was true love.

Nothing can deceive a woman who loves. She is a most delicate thermometer, and registers the fluctuating temperature of passion with minutest accuracy. An inflection of the voice, the turn of a sentence, are indications to her of the growing or lessening tenderness of her lover, which she will detect before he himself is conscious of any change of feeling. Her intuition is marvellous. It may be true that men are deceivers ever; yet women are rarely deceived. They are forsaken and betrayed, because passion weakens, not the judgment, but the will to act upon it.

Kate was silent for a few moments, and then replied, in the low but clear and firm tones which were habitual with her, "It may be unwomanly to speak so frankly, but I confess I do love you, Fred, as I always have done, and always shall do."

Fred recoiled a little at the calm deliberation of her words.

"You know," she went on, "that my life has not been very happy. I have experienced, it is true, nothing which ought to make one unhappy. But ever since I was a little child I have craved for a warmer and closer sympathy than those around me could give. My mother is very kind to me, but her ways and her nature are not mine, and it is because you seemed to understand me best that I have loved you so."

Her voice ended in a sob, and Fred, with a lump rising in his throat, drew her towards him tenderly.

But she quickly regained her composure, and began again, "Now you will at least believe that what I'm going to say to you is sincere. I know you better than you know yourself. You are, I'm sure, very fond of me. But that is not enough. The dearest wish of your heart is to enter public life, and to win a great name for yourself. Your father is trying to find for you a seat in

Parliament, and has built all his hopes on your success as a member. Now, no man can serve loyally two masters, or two mistresses either. You, Fred, have chosen Fame, and you must serve her. We're neither of us very rich, and if we married you might be compelled to abandon your ambition. I dare not put your love to such a test."

Fred interrupted with a vehement protest.

She quietly stopped him. "I'm quite sure you would give up your prospects and marry me, but, dear, I'm also sure that you would live to repine. I am a hasty-tempered and jealous woman, and if, as my husband, you should regret the sacrifice you made for me, we should neither of us be happy. No, Fred; if, by and by, when your position is assured, you find that you've made no mistake, and that you really do love me, I will become your wife, for I shall never marry any one else. But I love you too much to run any risks."

At that moment Fred was nearer to real love than he had ever been in his life. He drew her to him, and passionately kissed her lips; nor did she resist.

Then, with a happy laugh, she disengaged herself and said, "Let us go home; it's quite dark; and, after all, I haven't told you about my magician, Mr. Arnitte."

CHAPTER II

MRS. WYNNSTON sat in her low easy-chair before the fire, and awaited the arrival of her guests. She was tall and well proportioned, and possessed what a brilliant novelist has described as a " presence." Perhaps she was five feet six or seven inches in height, but if you had seen her by the side of a lady with half a head more you would have declared her to be the taller. This was the effect of the " presence." Like most wines, and unlike most women, she had improved with age. She had entirely outgrown an early *penchant* for eau de Cologne and fainting fits. An interest

had come into her life which, as a wife
and a young widow, she lacked, and that
interest centred in the ancient, dilapidated,
and ill-attended church in which such of
the rustic inhabitants as rejected the minis-
trations of a Methodist tailor sought the
means of grace.

Ten years ago her father, the owner of Lorton House, died, and, leaving no son behind
him, bequeathed his modest property to his
only surviving daughter. Mrs. Wynnston,
leaving the Midland house of her brother-in-
law, returned to the Northern home of her
birth. Then it was that an opportunity offered
itself to her such as a woman rarely neglects,
and she ceased to be hysterical and became
evangelical.

The estimable pagan whom Providence and
the patron of the living had called to be vicar

of Lorton was not in the best odour in Lorton
society. For one thing, he had quarrelled
with his wife—a terrible shrew—and Society
always regards a parson who lives apart from
his wife as a rather doubtful character. But
he might have lived down calumny had he
not been the brother of a baronet who owned
half the country-side. Now, the grandees of
Lorton had plenty of money; but, alas! what
they had they had made. The vicar of Lorton
cherished strong opinions on the subject of
wealth. On one occasion he preached upon
the difficulty which a rich man is said to experience in entering the Kingdom of Heaven.
He began by delicately hinting that, so far as
he was concerned, the acceptance of any kingdom outside the realms of terrestrial experience
was a matter of professional rather than personal belief. But, for the purposes of the

moment, premising the existence of a Kingdom of Heaven, or, indeed, a celestial government of any kind, he was fully convinced that rich men would find it hard to secure the approval of that administration, not because of the evil uses to which they put their wealth when they had acquired it, but rather because of the contemptible tricks they resorted to to make it. Hence, people of birth, who enjoyed the advantages conferred upon their ancestors, male and female, by grateful monarchs for services rendered, might possess their riches with untroubled spirits, assured that they would find their way into Abraham's bosom with as little difficulty as the raggedest Lazarus ever transferred to the paternal care of the patient and somewhat to be pitied patriarch. Incidentally the reverend gentleman remarked that Dives was probably a Phœnician shipowner, a Samarian wine-grower, a Jewish lawyer in large practice, or perhaps a Gentile tax-collector. The one thing certain was that he was not a member of an old family, or he never would have found himself on the wrong side of the gulf.

The vicar's theology was perhaps questionable, but his astronomy was perfect. The injunction to search the Scriptures he complacently ignored; but then every fine night he searched the heavens through a six-inch refractor. Nothing in the universe touched his imagination and kindled his enthusiasm like the study of the heavenly bodies. It is reported that one Sunday morning he coolly announced, after publishing the banns of marriage between two of his parishioners, "There will be an eclipse of the moon this

evening, and therefore no service will be held
to-night in this church, in order that the
congregation may have an opportunity of
witnessing a very interesting natural pheno-
menon." Neither his want of reverence nor
his ill-disguised scepticism, however, offended
his congregation. They, good people, would
listen with a delightful shiver of apprehension, an exquisite presentiment of spiritual
danger, to a plain intimation from the pulpit
that the book of Genesis was all nonsense,
that Adam and Eve were the rather weak
and somewhat improper creatures of barbar-
ous imagination, that Eden was about as real
as El Dorado, and Moses himself probably
nothing but a sun-myth. These things did
not distress the people of Lorton, who felt,
perhaps, that in the final arbitration any
little shortcomings of their own might be

successfully attributed to the evil example and pernicious. doctrines of their pastor. What finally drove them away was the reverend gentleman's intellectual pride. So long as he contented himself with contradicting the apostles and ridiculing the prophets they pitied and forgave him. But they could not pardon or forget his insolence to themselves. He would insist on preaching science to them instead of the gospel. When they failed to comprehend him they were secretly humiliated, and when, after laboriously explaining some rudimentary proposition, he would lean forward and remark, with his sweetest smile, "Even *you* can understand that," they felt openly insulted. Providence, they plaintively declared, had not bestowed upon every one the advantages of a university education, and to sneer at a man because he could not sum $x + 1$ to the nth, or had never heard of Kepler's law, was like casting an imputation upon the wisdom and benevolence of Heaven. One by one they dropped off, most of them transferring their patronage to a church three miles away, where the doctrine was more orthodox and the parson more polite. The squire was the first to go. He was not the real squire—only a poor makeshift, a retired banker, who rented the hall from its absentee proprietor, and who had fondly hoped to take on hire also the privileges and authority of a county magnate. He was a disagreeable, purse-proud person, and the vicar cordially detested him. One Saturday they came to high words on the subject of scientific rose-growing—a matter on which the squire claimed to be an authority, because he kept three gardeners.

Next day the vicar preached an edifying dis-course on the ejection of the money-changers from the temple, drawing the lesson that if the Church acted in the spirit of her Divine Master she would exclude from her com-munion all who lived on usury and derived a dishonourable income from compound in-terest. The squire was never more seen within the doors of Lorton Church, but, with a fine sense of irony, he insisted that his prominent square pew should be occupied at every service by his kitchenmaids and other under-servants.

When Mrs. Wynnston went to live at Lorton the congregation consisted of a few villagers and the servants of the departed pew-owners. Mrs. Wynnston saw her oppor-tunity. Like Cæsar, who preferred to be first in a petty hamlet rather than second in

Rome, she chose to rule in Lorton Church rather than serve in a more popular and important place of worship. She at once assumed the position and the dignity of a lady-patroness, and the first person she patronised was the vicar. Of the true beauty of holiness Mrs. Wynnston had nothing, but she was a great stickler for propriety. The vicar's surplice was decidedly antique. Many washings had imparted to it a subtle tone, in which gray, yellow, and brown seemed struggling for the mastery. Mrs. Wynnston suggested that a new one would be an improvement. The vicar blandly acquiesced, but appeared as before in his venerable garment. Mrs. Wynnston wrote to London for a surplice built on the latest and most approved lines, and sent it and the bill to the reverend gentleman. The vicar wore the one and paid the other, and from that moment was the bondslave of Mrs. Wynnston. He rather enjoyed his captivity. It amused him. For the interests of his church he himself cared little, and to be driven into manifestations of consuming zeal by a woman whose ecclesiastical enthusiasm was only a hobby seemed to him charmingly comical. In one way Mrs. Wynnston's patronage was very congenial to him. To her he tacitly consigned the spiritual and temporal charge of the parish. While he, in all contentment, shut himself up among his roses and his telescopes, she gave alms to the poor, visited the sick, sought out the wandering, and, but for an absurd canonical prejudice against women, would have taken the chair at the vestry meetings. The vicar, indeed, had once, with the gravest of faces, hinted that a special episcopal dispensation might open to her ambition the honourable office of churchwarden. But nothing came of the idea. She was successful in most of her aims. The village lads touched their caps to her, and the village girls dropped curtseys. She disposed of the charitable funds of the church, chose the hymns and tunes on Sundays, frequently suggested the texts, and might, with the vicar's great goodwill, have preached on them too, if the law ·had only permitted it. In one thing, however, she completely failed. Her efforts to bring about a reconciliation between the vicar and the righteously-offended magnates of Lorton only involved her in the reverend gentleman's unpopularity, and the circle which frequented her drawing-room was consequently limited in number.

The vicar was the first to arrive, and he and Mrs. Wynnston at once plunged into an edifying conversation upon the effeminate affectations of the modern clergy.

"Now, you remember," said the reverend gentleman, "the young fellow who came over from Longdale to preach for me the Sunday before last. He's six feet high, was stroke in his college boat two years ago, and thrashed every boxing - man at Oxford. When he arrived on Saturday night he sat up with me smoking his pipe and drinking whisky until midnight, and would persist in talking athletics—a subject which I detest. When he went away on Monday morning I am certain he 'chucked' my housemaid, Mary, under the chin, and indeed I suspect that along with half-a-crown he gave her a kiss."

Mrs. Wynnston looked appropriately shocked.

"Yet," continued the vicar, "you saw and heard the young donkey at morning service. As soon as he was in his surplice he put on a sweet and languishing smile, just as a prima donna screws her face into amiable contortions as she runs on the stage to sing, and in a voice which seemed to come down his nose from the crown of his head he began his idiotic whining in the vestry."

The vicar's pale face flushed with angry contempt.

"And then," he went on, "what an absurd performance he made of the lessons! Why in the world it should be more respectful, or more acceptable to Providence, to sound the 'ed' to every past tense and participle in the Bible I never could understand. I could scarcely contain myself as he read, or rather snivelled, 'And he talk-ed with the woman, and she pleas-ed Samson well. And after a while he return-ed to take her, and he turn-ed aside to see the carcase of the lion.' Such affectations, both of tone, pronunciation, and demeanour, are peculiar to the English clergy. As far as my experience goes, you never find them among dissenting ministers, or Romish priests whom many of our young parsons attempt to ape. There is too much spiritual earnestness among the former, and too much historic dignity among the latter, to permit of such absurd displays."

Kate and Fred chatted at the other side of the room, undisturbed by the vicar's vehement denunciations—she, radiant and happy, casting away, as only a woman can, all her instinctive forebodings; he, flattered and contented by the undisguised affection and admiration of a handsome and attractive young woman.

"By the way," she said, "we have a surprise for you. You recollect our old playmate, Mary O'Connor? You should do, for she was your little sweetheart."

Fred ventured to make a mild denial.

"Nonsense; any one who saw how red and stupid you became whenever she was near could have told it. Well, she and her brother, whom we never knew, are staying for the summer at a farmhouse near the village. They called on mamma, and she asked them to dine with us to-night. Now, I wonder whether you'll blush and stammer when Mary comes in, as you used to do." Kate laughed, but Fred thought he detected a trace of anxiety in her features.

"You're the only person now," he whispered, "before whom I shall blush and stammer."

"Humph," was the reply, "I haven't seen much modest agitation about you so far. But perhaps you'll improve. Who knows?"

The arrival of the guests interrupted the *tête-à-tête*, and when Mr. and Miss O'Connor were announced Fred, under the mischievous eye of Kate, conducted himself with becoming composure. As for Mary O'Connor, no ordinary event of life could have ruffled her serene tranquillity. She had grown into an extraordinarily beautiful woman. Her face and figure were those of a Greek statue of the best period. As she stood for an instant talking with his aunt Fred's memory flashed to a long corridor of the Louvre, and he remembered how, one gray afternoon, he found himself for the first time looking down a vista of noble figures at the divine loveliness of the Venus of Milo. An intense side light and a dark background threw the statue which faced him into strong relief. He walked with hesitating steps towards it, fearing lest a closer approach should dissipate the sense of pure and perfect proportion which filled him. He had never before experienced that feeling of almost religious awe and exaltation which perfection of form sometimes excites in natures susceptible of artistic emotion. He recollected how, after a long and reverent survey of the Venus, the rest of the statues seemed to him so clumsy and unattractive that he speedily left the building. Now he underwent a similar mental experience.

His eye fell upon Kate, and he suddenly became aware that her figure was somewhat "dumpy."

The last arrival was Mr. Arnitte, and Fred, whose left - hand neighbour he was at the dinner - table, furtively studied the man of mystery who had astonished his ingenuous cousin. He was a slender man, of middle height, with long limbs, loose joints, and a certain awkwardness, both of action and repose. His head and face proclaimed him to be a man of no ordinary character. His features were of a slightly Semitic cast. His skin was extremely dark and sallow, but clear. His wavy hair, worn rather long, had the blue-black sheen of a raven's wing. His forehead was remarkably high and broad, with strongly-marked veins, and a portentous knit between the brows. His nose was very

large and prominent, its shape suggesting
aggressiveness, and its dilating nostrils passion. His constant expression was that
of carefully-prepared inscrutability, through
which a watchful self-consciousness showed.
He was evidently either an artificial man, or
a man playing an artificial part. His face
and figure reminded Fred of a well-known
English statesman, and Fred fancied, from a
curious curl which he wore, and from his
tricks of face, manner, and voice, that he was
conscious of, and cultivated, the resemblance.
His voice was as peculiar as his appearance.
It was rasping and unmusical, but extremely
expressive. Though not loud, it dominated
all conversation, and when Mr. Arnitte spoke
every one else stopped talking and began to
listen. He was a well-informed man, who
appeared to have been everywhere and known

everybody.   His conversation was bright and easy, and made piquant by an artistic dash of cynicism.   What he said was rarely brilliant, but always so said as to seem brilliant. Mrs. Wynnston, with the instinct of a hostess, made a mental memorandum that Mr. Arnitte was a man who earned his dinner.   Down the table he exchanged amusing banter with the vicar, while Fred, watching, mechanically noted that he had a large, dark, powerful hand, with fingers of great length, gnarled knuckles, and well-shaped filbert nails. There was something remorseless and uncanny about that hand, and it filled Fred with an uneasy sense that he had somewhere heard or read about one like it.

There was a pause in the conversation, and Arnitte's eye glanced for an instant, with an amused twinkle, on Fred.   He immediately bent forward and said "Wordsworth's line in Coleridge's *Ancient Mariner*, 'Long and lank, and brown, as is the ribbed sea sand.'" Then, without noticing Fred's start of astonishment, he went on: "Do you know that line is a puzzle to me? How ought one to punctuate it? Should it be 'Long,—and lank,—and brown,—as is the ribbed sea sand,' or 'Long and lank,—and brown as is the ribbed sea sand?' The latter reading makes the simile more strictly appropriate, yet, I think, somehow it weakens it."

Before he ceased Fred broke in, "Really, I don't know which is the better. But do you mind telling me how you managed to conjecture that I was searching about my memory for that line?"

Arnitte laughed. "If I were going to found a religion, or intended to appear as a public performer, I should say without hesitation that I had read your thoughts. As I have no such intentions, I don't mind confessing that I'm as much in the dark as yourself."

The vicar was heard dilating to Mrs. Wynnston upon the curiosities of coincidence and the mathematical principles of the rule of " Probabilities."

Arnitte interrupted. "Perhaps you're right. Perhaps it was a curious coincidence. Yet I know what you're thinking at the present moment. The word 'charlatan' is in your mind now."

The quick flush which sprang to the vicar's fresh face was a plain confession that Arnitte had again hit the mark. But the reverend gentleman looked frankly up the table and replied, "Believe me, though the word may have passed through my mind, my judgment never applied it."

Arnitte courteously bowed.

"And if," continued the vicar, "I said 'curious coincidence' before, I am now tempted to say, 'clever conjecture.'"

"Well," was the reply, "I hardly know myself. Did you ever read Edgar Poe's weird story of the two friends who were walking along the streets of Paris when one broke a long pause by answering a question which the other was mentally asking? The mind-reader afterwards explained the process by which he had followed the thoughts of his friend, and traced each step by which his delicate powers of observation and quick associations of ideas had produced the surprising result. Yet, I don't know that the explanation is quite satisfying. Now, I certainly saw that Mr. Hazzleden was looking at my hand, and in some way I felt assured, from the expression of inquiry on his face, that he was trying to recollect Wordsworth's line, which I must say is applicable," and he laughingly held up his hand.

"Yet," he continued, "I cannot trace, as Poe does, the complete process which revealed to me Mr. Hazzleden's thoughts."

The vicar quoted Hume on the antecedent improbability of miracles, asserting, with evident relish, that it was more prudent to believe in the error or dishonesty of any person or number of persons than in the possession by any one of powers pronounced by the general experience of men to be supernatural. "Of course," he went on, "the theory doesn't quite meet your difficulty, for you have fallen into no error, and made no unjustifiable claim. But, if you read every secret thought of every person here to-night, I should marvel at the wonders of coincidence and your acuteness in conjecture, rather than attribute to you a faculty different in kind, as well as degree, from those possessed by myself and the majority of mankind."

"As a scientific man," returned Arnitte thoughtfully, "you would be quite right;" and, after a pause,—"Yet I sometimes think, in a vague, half-reasoning way, that modern science is altogether on the wrong track."

The vicar raised his eyebrows, and almost imperceptibly shrugged his shoulders.

Arnitte went on : "I cannot, I fear, make myself perfectly clear. You are a distinguished astronomer. Now, do you not think that science takes too much account of the heavenly bodies, and too little of the consciousness of those who observe them ? There is no worth or value, intellectual or moral, in a star, or its properties, apart from the effect produced on human minds. Is it not Arnold who has pointed out that knowledge is useless unless correlated with conduct ?"

The vicar laughed unpleasantly. " I thought," he said, " when you began, that you were going to preach from the gospel according to St. Matthew Arnold. It is lamentable to contemplate the injury to science which that man's ignorance and prejudice have done."

" Please don't condemn me yet," pleaded Arnitte modestly. " I was unwise to meddle with the Arnold argument, inasmuch as my personal objection to the methods of science lies in another direction. Again, take the case of your own studies. What are the heavens really to you ?   Certainly not billions of miles of space and thousands of suns and systems !   They are an impression received through two tiny specks in your eyes, and registered in some form or other in your mind.   You cannot begin to prove that the impression has any objective reality."

An ejaculation was rising to the vicar's lips, but Arnitte hastily went on : " You are going to say that I'm now lost in a quagmire of transcendentalism.   But I think you're wrong.   I neither dispute nor doubt the reality of our impressions.   All I do is to point out that they are impressions, and that science contemptuously refuses to study the methods by which, and the medium through which, they are received.   Knowledge is not external fact, of which we have positive cognisance, but the reaction of external fact upon human faculties. And yet men of science think it unphilosophical to study and endeavour to understand thoroughly those faculties before professing to examine so-called 'natural phenomena.' It seems to me that if we were half as ready to study and develop our own powers as we are to acquire what we are pleased to call 'objective facts,' our ideas in many ways would receive valuable correction."

The vicar was preparing a crushing rejoinder when Mrs. Wynnston rose, and the conversation was broken off. Nor was it again renewed. The departure of the ladies was followed by that curious relaxing of bodies and minds which is always noticeable after a dinner-party. Man is a dual creature. When seated by the side of a woman he belongs to one species; when the woman has risen and gone away he belongs to another. The same change is rarely noticeable in the female sex; but there is something akin to it in the change which takes place in a woman when she puts off her everyday attire and dons her ball dress. The hostess, however, leads from the table to the drawing-room the same beings who sat at it. Those who are left behind are metamorphosed. There is an apparent throwing off of restraint; the host and his friends stretch their limbs and adopt such attitudes as please them most. Cigars are lighted, and wine is swallowed in greater gulps. The whole atmosphere of the room has changed.

Neither Arnitte nor the vicar was disposed to revert to metaphysics. The former was disputing with Fred the precise spot in the Alps from whence the finest view is to be obtained. The latter was speculating with O'Connor upon the prospects of a dissolution of Parliament, and of the effects which an appeal to the country would have on the question of disestablishment.

Presently the notes of a rich contralto voice reached the room, and Fred began to fidget. To his great inward satisfaction most of the men threw away their cigars, and a move was made to the drawing-room, where Mary O'Connor, accompanying herself on the piano, was singing an exquisitely sweet and pathetic air from an oratorio. The intense feeling which this girl manifested deeply moved Fred, who thought he had never heard anything so beautiful in his life. Kate played badly and sang worse—a circumstance which troubled him, for he was unusually susceptible to the influence of music. It was his comfort in grief, his occupation in idleness, his friend in happiness. He sometimes, during the few days of their dubious engagement, had felt this deficiency in Kate very acutely. If he asked her to play she would strum an imbecile waltz; if he asked her to sing she would frolic through the latest absurdity from a comic opera. Now the gracious tones of Mary O'Connor's voice filled him with a mingled sentiment of delight and distress, which he carefully refrained from analysing.

Later in the evening some one asked Arnitte to sing. He at once consented, and, walking to the piano, rubbed his large hands together, and executed a brilliant pyrotechnical prelude, which ended in a sequence of chromatic harmonies. Then he began to sing, in a strong and nervous baritone voice :—

" The morning comes, and the tempest
  Roars from the wild North-West,
And its moaning mocks the moaning
  Of a heart that can find no rest.
Oh ! daylight, how fondly I seek thee,
  While dashed on the window-pane
I see, in the first gray dawning,
  The tears of a falling rain.

" The broad noon comes, and the sunbeams
  Sparkle on lake and lea ;
But the passing breath from the mountain
  Whispers no peace to me.
The glare of the midday passes,
  The fierce light fades at last,
But time cannot temper the memories
  That beat from the pitiless past.

" The faint eve falls, and a glory
  Crimsons the glowing west ;
The sighing song of wind and sea
  Hushes the world to rest.
Oh, darkness ! I call thee to cover
  The phantoms of hopes long dead,
Till life's stern struggle is over,
  Till Death's swift arrow has sped."

Fred fancied that as the song drew to
an end Arnitte's voice became very harsh, as

though proceeding from a dry throat, and
when the singer finished and swung round
on the piano-stool his face was paler than
usual; and Fred noticed, or thought he
noticed, that his eye rested with a strange
flash on O'Connor, sitting at the other end
of the room talking to Kate.

Fred mechanically wondered whether the
song was very fine or melodramatic rubbish,
but he said to Arnitte, "That's a very effec-
tive song.   Whom is it by?"

"I don't know who wrote the words," was
the reply; "I found them in a newspaper.
The setting is my own.   It seemed to me to
fit the words, and I wrote it down when it
occurred to me."

Again Fred was surprised, and a couple of
hours afterwards, when in bed, he tossed
about, wondering whether this man, who

seemed both to attract and repel him, was a genius or a quack. Other doubts also would creep into his mind, but he steadily refused to consider them. All that was certain to him was that he was physically and mentally depressed, and that sleep would not come to his relief.

CHAPTER III

DURING his residence at Lorton O'Connor had struck up an acquaintance with a young fellow named Phillips, the son of a farmer. Richard Phillips, the girls of the village always declared, "looked like a gentleman." He himself was very much of their opinion, and his father, sharing in the prevalent belief, determined to make him one. The lad was a weak creature, with a fair, pretty face, languid, nerveless limbs, a flabby body, and a flabby mind. He was ridiculously vain and boastful; and, having by some chance penetrated into the fringe of the "genteel society" of Lorton, considered himself a great deal too refined for the companionship of the sons and daughters of farmers. He had served an apprenticeship to a solicitor in a neighbouring market-town. Now, nearly five and twenty years of age, he was idling away his time in his father's house, waiting for something to turn up, and complacently assured that fortune was secretly contriving for him a very distinguished destiny.

Phillips was nearly enthusiastic over one hobby, and that was boating. He was, indeed, an expert amateur sailor, and it was in some excursion on the bay that O'Connor and his sister had first met him. O'Connor's gray eyes were keenly observant. He measured and weighed the young man's character in the first week of their acquaintanceship. Nor was he long in noting that

Phillips, with a weak man's timid audacity, had fallen over ears in love with Mary. O'Connor's private opinions as to the advisability of transforming his new friend into a brother-in-law he scrupulously kept to himself. But he manifested on all occasions to the romantic Richard a cordiality and frankness unusual in a man of his sullen and silent disposition, and appeared to seek opportunities of cultivating the young man's friendship, and of throwing him into the society of his sister.

O'Connor and his friend made many excursions among the heather-clad hills around Lorton. One morning the pair had climbed an easy summit, and, sitting in a little hollow sheltered from the wind, were looking down upon a pleasant winding valley which lay shimmering beneath them in the heat of a noonday sun.

A poet has written of "the sleep that is among the lonely hills." Viewed from the hills the vales seem to sleep too. Below there may be busy life and noise and bustle. Yet, look down from heights above, so small a thing is human action, and all seems still. The worker in the fields, a tiny speck, is no longer a conscious being, with parts and powers and will, living and loving and toiling; a troop of laughing boys, racing along the fields yonder, are only as leaves dancing before the breeze; the country cart, creaking along that white road, has ceased to be a common and convenient contrivance for carrying potatoes to market. The perspective of things is changed. Man no longer stands at the "point of sight," and life is swallowed up in nature.

A stream ran along the bottom of the

valley, and O'Connor, directed by the out-stretched hand of Phillips, was trying to discern a little white bridge, from the arch of which his companion had hooked a five-pound trout.

Presently a puff of steam floated lazily from out of a line of distant trees, and a far-off whistle announced the progress of the mid-day mail speeding away to the north. Only a railway can break the sleep that falls on and from the lonely hills.

Phillips made some conventional protest against the nineteenth century barbarism which ruins the lovely valleys of England, that directors may earn salaries and share-holders draw dividends.

" I never can see," replied O'Connor, " that railways detract from the picturesqueness of a landscape. They make towns noisy and dirty, but I rather like to see the track stretching away through a pretty country; and I never think that a train, at any rate seen from a distance, is an ugly object. I have been in places in the west of America where I should have thought a locomotive, with all its suggestions of life and industry, the most beautiful thing which could cross the landscape."

Phillips had read Ruskin, and looked shocked.

"Besides," continued O'Connor, his face darkening, "I am an Irishman. What would I not give to have these engines, dragging trade and wealth and happiness after them, through the valleys of my own country?"

There was a pause. Phillips gazed down the valley, and O'Connor dug a hole in the turf with his walking-stick.

Presently he resumed : " Phillips, I know
I may trust you.   My sister Mary and I "—
he stole a keen glance at the young man—
" my sister Mary and I are here in England
on a sacred mission.   We do not love you
English, though some of you we think not
unworthy to be our friends.   We were born,
both of us, in Ireland, the children of a
farmer who drew from his land enough to
live honestly, to clothe himself and us, and
to pay a fair rent.   It was rather poor,
stony land, and one winter, when Mary was
a very little girl, and I was just big enough
to do odd jobs on the farm, a bright idea
occurred to my father.   Together we set to
work to carry it out.   On bitter cold and
wet days we went out as soon as it was
light, and trudged over the rough land,
and gathered up all the stones we could

find, and carried them, and piled them up in heaps at the back of the cottage. It took us two months to clear the fields, which our grandfathers for generations before us—sensible men—had thought good enough as they were. Then, for another month, in every moment we could spare from digging and sowing, we turned builders, and before the spring was upon us we had run up a low wall round the yard and a new place for the pigs."

O'Connor's voice grew harsher and louder as he went on, and he beat the grass at his feet with his stick.

"In the spring the agent came for his rent. We only saw him four times a year; he lived twenty miles off, and we were away up in the hills. He collected money for a rich nobleman—nobleman! Phillips—the owner of the soil which my fathers had tilled for centuries. I never saw him, scarcely knew his name. He was said to live somewhere in England, in a palace built of gold, and hung with silk, and sparkling with jewels. As a lad I often wondered what this place could be like, and how one would feel always to have a fire when one was cold, and bread when one was hungry, and a bed to sleep on instead of straw. I have seen this great mansion since, and found that it was built, not of gold, but of human flesh, mortared with human blood. I have seen the great nobleman. He is a decrepit old drunkard."

O'Connor paused again, as if choked. Then he went on: "The agent came, and my father proudly showed him our winter's work. I can see now—may God Almighty curse him!—the sly smile on the scoundrel's face. He jingled the keys in his pocket, and asked many questions: how long the work had taken us, whether it was fatiguing, if we found the new pig-sty convenient, and if the land promised any great improvement. Then he said, in his soft voice, 'Well, you seem to have done a good stroke of business. I shall only double the rent, and charge you a fair price for building materials. Of course you had no right to use the landlord's stones without his permission; and if you don't like to pay you can put them back where you found them.' My father, soft-hearted fellow, thought of his children, and began to cry. My mother went down on her knees in the mud of the farmyard, and prayed for mercy from the saints and from him. The saints, however, seemed to be otherwise engaged just then, and the agent rode off, calling back, 'Ta, ta! I don't want to be hard on you. I'll give you six months to pay for the stone.' That year the blight fell on the potatoes. All the crops were a failure. My father sold the pigs to get money to pay for the stone. But all his labour and all his savings were not sufficient to pay the double-rent. In the autumn we were evicted. The cottage was set on fire by the agent's orders, and our little household goods—God knows, few and poor enough !—were burned. That winter we lived and starved in a hut of boughs and mud built in a ditch by my father and me. Not a soul dared lend us a helping hand, but on dark nights a neighbouring farmer would steal up and leave us a bit of turf and a few potatoes. In that hut my mother was confined, and both she and the baby died. My father begged, or stole—I don't know which—a few boards, and made a coffin for them, and a poor priest buried them for a shilling, which our old neighbours subscribed, on the edge of the bog, as the nearest churchyard was seven miles away, and we could get no one to help to carry the coffin. Soon after Mary, my sister, took ill with famine fever, and we were fast becoming too weak to tramp ten miles to the seashore and back to get seaweed to boil and eat. One day, when we thought little Mary was dying, an Englishman, a doctor, rode by. What he was doing in that wild country in the winter I never knew. He was a good man, and for his sake I hope that some may be spared from the curse which will pursue the English nation in this world and the next, if there is one. He stopped a whole week in our hovel, and nursed the child himself till she was fit to be moved. Then he gave

money to my father to take him and me to
America. But he had come to love the sweet
face of my sister. He was an old man, with
neither wife nor child. He offered to take
her to his home in England, and to love and
cherish her as his own daughter. My father
consented, and we found that there was one
true and tender Englishman, for he kept his
word till he died, and then left his little
fortune to Mary. They lived near to the
Hazzledens, and that is how my sister came
to know young Hazzleden. They were very
fond of one another as children,"—he spoke
in a questioning tone, and again scrutinised
the young man; "but Mary is a true Irish-
woman. Her whole heart is in the cause.
She has devoted all her means to it, and she
will never love a man who is not one of us,
in sympathy, if not in birth."

"How did you get on in America?"
Phillips asked.

"Everything prospered with us. We
went West; we obtained a large concession
of land, and our generous friend, to whom
my father had written, helped us to buy a
little stock. Money seemed to grow under
our hands. We paid our debt to our bene-
factor, and I paid mine to our old agent."

"How?" said Phillips.

"Well, one fine evening he was found dead
on the road, with a bullet in his heart."

Phillips shrank away from the side of his
companion.

"Oh!" laughed the Irishman, "don't
think I shot the ruffian, though I would
have done so had I ever met him. I only
sent a hundred pounds to a certain society of
which I had heard while in New York, and

to an officer of which I told our story. I
have not the least idea who murdered the
fellow. But, to make a long tale short, in
eight years' time we were independent, if not
rich. My father died, and I sold off the
ranche at once, and went to Boston. I had
always felt, Phillips, that to influence one's
fellows one must have some education and
social culture. I had read as much as I
could, and was not absolutely ignorant of the
'humanities.'" He laughed, as though the
word amused him. "I entered at Harvard,
and my money got me into a fairly good set
in the city. A year later I travelled through
the South, to mend my manners, among the
Virginian aristocrats. Oh, I met plenty of
fine people, and had a very good time. Then
Mary's old friend died, and I came over and
taught her my plans, and inspired her with

my ideas. Don't you think we make a very pretty pair of conspirators?"

Phillips babbled some words of assent.

"Yes," resumed the Irishman, "whatever wealth and ability we possess we have devoted to the service of Ireland. Your country has shown no mercy to mine for five hundred years. You have used it as a tool, you have robbed it, you have oppressed it, you have slaughtered its people, you have crushed its trade, you have turned its fields into a desert, you have never done one good thing to Ireland for Ireland's sake, and now the hour of retribution has come, and we are its ministers. Go and tell your police, your magistrates, your rulers; they will give much for the bodies of Mary and me."

There was careful study in all this rant. O'Connor, while seeming to open his heart to

Phillips, had really told him nothing, except
that he had been concerned in the death of
the agent. Into this confession he had
slipped unawares, and his subsequent wild-
ness was partly assumed in the hope of
blurring the recollection of that unfortunate
admission.

Phillips was simply dazed. He had come
to worship Mary with all the fervour of his
weak nature, and to lean with quite a fra-
ternal confidence upon O'Connor,—and they
were Irish revolutionaries, probably assassins
and "dynamitards." A stronger man would
have been troubled. But what to do? He
could not abandon his hopes of Mary were
she ten times an Irish conspirator. Doubt-
less she was under the influence of her
brother, and he, poor fellow, was clearly
a monomaniac. His early sufferings had

affected his brain. He must be humoured,
and, if possible, weaned from his mad pro-
jects.

They strolled down the zigzag hillside
paths, and Phillips, as he thought, with
infinite address, soothed O'Connor, and at
the same time drew from him his designs.

"I know it is hard," the latter remarked,
"to compel justice from thirty millions of
people for the benefit of five. You have all
the warlike resources, the wealth, the num-
bers; yet we are not quite helpless. I have
looked down twenty feet through the water
of an American bay to the white sand,
and I have seen a pulpy creature, which
somehow always reminded me of a fat,
over-fed, apoplectic city man—perhaps an
alderman. It had no scales, no teeth, and
no powerful jaws. Apparently the Creator

forgot to give it either the means of fighting or running away. Presently a fish, alert and fierce, swift as a swallow and savage as a vulture, would see, through its horrible cruel eyes, the wretched alderman lying on the sand. A dozen other ugly brutes, all with murderous intent, would glide, from heaven knows where, towards that big-bellied old glutton. By the way, don't you think there is something creepy about the noiseless motion of a fish, especially when he is darting down on his prey? Well, all these hungry fishes would glide towards the 'alderman,' who never moved a muscle, and you, of course, expected in a few seconds to find the assassins quarrelling over the pieces. Not a bit of it. Before the swiftest of the gang could reach our friend a dense black cloud spread all round him through the water.   It looked very nasty, and you could easily imagine that it smelled and tasted very nasty.   The first fish dashed quickly into it, but dashed out again even quicker. You could see that that fish was sick.   His stomach couldn't stand the black stuff.   The other fishes would try their luck, but all with the same result.   Some, desperate for their dinners, would go into the nauseous stuff three or four times, till they rolled over on their backs and floated, either dead or stupefied.   By and by, when all was quiet again, the old fellow would wobble out of his abominable cloud and go, I suppose, off home. The illustration is not complimentary, but, upon my word, Phillips, I never saw that fish without thinking that Ireland is not so help-less as people suppose.   She has no teeth and jaws—but muskets and ironclads are not the only offensive and defensive resources of civilisation."

They had reached O'Connor's door. "Won't you lunch with us?" he said to Phillips. The young man hesitated, then with an embarrassed smile plunged through the doorway. O'Connor, who had closely watched his hesitation, could not repress a sigh of relief as he followed his friend into the house.

CHAPTER IV

FRED was anything but happy. Lorton House, with its low rooms, its heavy hangings, and its ancient furniture, oppressed him. The society of his aunt and cousin wearied him. He would have started on a cruise, or gone home, or gone anywhere, but for two reasons. One was that he had engaged himself to Kate, and could not in common civility cut short his visit without a very good excuse; and the other was that he did not at the bottom of his heart desire to leave Lorton just then. He was attentive and affectionate to Kate. They strolled about the lanes together, they made excursions in the pony phaeton, Kate driving, Fred lolling at once listlessly and restlessly at her side. They played tennis together on the lawn, but Fred never proposed another stroll down the Apple Walk to the shore. He knew that Kate's eyes would sparkle, that she would nestle caressingly at his side, if he suggested another evening chat at the dingle. He secretly wondered if he should ever again think Kate so irresistibly lovable as he did that night when, with full heart and honest conviction, he asked her to be his wife. He constantly endeavoured to stifle all such thoughts, yet sometimes the consciousness would steal into his mind that down by the shore in the evening light, with her full eyes bent upon him, he should say and mean once more, "Kitty, darling, I love you."

But he never asked her to go. Was he sure that he wished to say and feel as on the first evening of his visit? Fred would have found it difficult to answer this question, and, after his wont, carefully abstained from putting it to himself.

Arnitte remained in the neighbourhood fishing, boating, riding, walking, and apparently enjoying to his heart's content a spell of outdoor life in glorious summer weather. Fred frequently encountered him, and was greatly attracted to him by his brilliant talk and by a sweet and ingratiating manner which he either manifested naturally or assumed with great success. He felt the need of male companionship to relieve the sense of tedium which was overmastering him. He would have preferred to be friendly with O'Connor, but that gentleman, while always

studiously polite, contrived, in ways which a
man of the world is never at a loss to discover, to check his advances. He had encountered Mary O'Connor riding out in the
cool of the morning two or three times, and
had had several pleasant talks over old times.
Fred, never an enthusiastic horseman, had
begun to ride out regularly before breakfast;
but at the end of a week Mary ceased to
appear in the narrow high-banked lane where
fern and bracken grew beneath the shelter of
the hedges, and which wound away down for
a mile to Lorton Church. Then Kate, who
could ride anything, and who only refrained
because her mother was nervous and kept
nothing in the stable but "a venerable family
pair," as Kate scornfully dubbed them, began
to hint at a morning gallop—"That is, Fred,"
she laughed, "if you can persuade mother's

fiery Arabians to go quicker than a walk."
But Fred's equestrian ardour had evaporated.
He said, "Oh yes, certainly," but the morning was always too hot, or it was too late, or
there was something else to do. He had
written to invite the O'Connors to an afternoon cruise in the *Sylph*, but as yet they
had sent no answer. Apparently they were
not eager to cultivate his acquaintance.

So he was thrown back upon Arnitte, and
a man more fitted to cure a friend of *ennui*
could not have been found. Arnitte fell into
the habit of calling at Lorton House in the
evening to play a set of tennis with Fred, or
perhaps against Fred and Kate, for he was
an expert at the game, and then to smoke a
cigar till dusk on a garden-seat which over-
looked the ravine and the bay beyond.

Insensibly Fred had been led to give his

new acquaintance a dozen little confidences. There was his engagement to Kate, which for some reason or other had not been announced. Mrs. Wynnston was just then too busy reorganising the church choir to think of anything else. Kate, of course, could not talk about it, and she had, moreover, no girl friends. Fred felt that it was a matter which in fairness to Kate ought to be made known, and would resolve over night to tell every one. But in the morning, if ever he thought about it, he would soliloquise, " Oh, everybody can see we're engaged, and besides, it's Aunt Wynnston's business to announce it." As the result, none of the friends who visited Lorton House had the smallest idea that Kate and Fred were engaged to be married.

But Arnitte found it out. Fred never

told him in so many words, and he, on his
part, never mentioned the subject. Yet Fred
knew perfectly well that Arnitte was aware
of his engagement. One evening Kate suggested a set at tennis. Fred, who was in
a contrary humour, refused. Kate pleaded,
Fred grew sullen, and in a minute a very
sharp quarrel was raging between the cousins.
The ominous red glow showed in Kate's eyes,
and she ended the incident by tossing her
racquet over the net and marching off to bed.
Fred whistled defiantly; and Arnitte, who
had been absorbed in the contemplation of a
common daisy at the far end of the lawn
which, alone out of all its family, the mowing
machine had spared, now slipped his arm
within Fred's and strolled to his favourite
seat. He chatted pleasantly, and soothed,
with all the art of a clever friend, the young

man's irritation. The conversation at length drifted to the subject of marriage.

Fred, completely won over, blurted out, " The difficulty always seems to me that one can never be sure a woman is—is——"

" Good enough for one," suggested Arnitte, blandly. " That's vanity."

" No, I didn't mean quite that; rather, whether she was suitable."

" Much the same thing," muttered Arnitte.

Without noticing the interruption Fred went on, " Perhaps it is vanity, or perhaps humility, or perhaps both. But I've always felt that to really love a woman a man should think her perfect. She should either be perfect, or his love should be strong enough to create a perfect delusion. What I doubt is whether some men—of course I am speaking generally," he added nervously. Arnitte nodded.—"What I doubt is whether every man can submit himself to such a lasting delusion. After marriage, or perhaps before, he begins to find out little faults of disposition and little blemishes of culture. He may even criticise the very face which once seemed nothing but beauty to him." Fred spoke with warmth, and, meeting Arnitte's laughing eye, coloured.

But the grave and kindly reply reassured him. "The moral of your observation and argument is, Hazzleden, that men should live in the world, and not in romantic visions. I don't think that because a man loves a woman he should take leave of his senses. You may as well seek for the philosopher's stone as for perfection of character. You know it doesn't exist, and you're a fool if you marry any woman with the expectation or even the faint hope of finding it. You and I have known each other for two or three weeks, and no doubt you, as a thinking man, have noticed faults in me, as I may have detected weaknesses in you. Do you think, then, that we could, either of us, marry a woman and go all through life under the belief that she was an angel?"

"That's just my point," interrupted Fred. "Of course I should find her out, and then I should feel that I didn't really love her."

"But why," said Arnitte, "should you ever begin the mistake? For my part, I don't believe in marrying angels. If it were possible it would be extremely unsatisfactory. A good woman is quite good enough for me. Besides, what proof of love can there be when the object is perfect? Now, my theory is this. A man falls in love with a woman partly through circumstances and partly of his free will. He feels that he needs her companionship and help and affection through life. He sees other women and, as a reasonable being, he admits that this one is more beautiful, that one better tempered, another plays the piano better, a fourth is more widely read or of keener intellect. He recognises these things just as he would see that this one is taller or that one darker. It is when he knows that his sweetheart or his wife has, like the rest of the world, faults and shortcomings, and still knows that she is necessary to him, that he is sure of the truth and strength of his love."

He rose and threw away his cigar. Fred followed him, and the pair strolled towards the house. Arnitte took his friend's arm and, after a pause, spoke again. " Hazzleden,

when I was a youth my elder brother was
drowned. He was engaged to a sweet young
girl, and one day they went boating on a
river near our house. The boat, we supposed, must have capsized from some cause
or other, and next day their bodies were
dragged up from the weeds at the bottom,
clasped in one another's arms. I remember
my mother's agony of grief, and how gray
and solemn for a while my own life seemed.
But my father never shed a tear, and when
some one spoke to him words of conventional
comfort only replied, 'Why should I sorrow?
The lad is happy to have died before he
found the earthen feet of his golden image.'
—'But do you think,' said his friend, 'the
image had earthen feet?'—'I do not know,'
answered my father; 'but I am quite sure at
some time or other he would have thought it

had.' The philosophy was false, Hazzleden, —false and yet true. Wise men do not search for golden images, then it is false; but if they do, ah!"—there was a quiver of pain in his voice—" then how true it is!"

Man is an abode of three chambers: there is the outer hall, where casual callers are received; there is the inner reception-room, where friends are welcomed and pass hours of loving intercourse; there is the secret inmost apartment, where no foot, however near and dear, ever may tread, where the man sits with his own soul. None else may know its angles, its recesses, how it is furnished, whether it is well appointed or squalid, whether it is bright or gloomy, whether it is garish or modest. Yet there are moments when the curtain before the door seems lifted for an instant and the eye of a friend may see, or fancy it sees, something of the sacred solitude. Fred imagined he had caught such a glimpse and unconsciously pressed Arnitte's arm.

The latter went on : "Don't dream dreams, Hazzleden, for you are certain to awaken; and don't covet too much happiness. I'm a heretic in most things, and I doubt whether happy men are the happiest. That sounds like a paradox, but it isn't. It's a good thing to be ground in the mills of God; to know what heartache is; to be crushed down—ay, even into the mud of life. Those who feed on sugar grow fat and stupid; the soul needs bitter tonics as well as the body. The men to whom the world owes most gratitude are not those who live in fairy gardens, but those who have sinned and suffered and sorrowed. A man shouldn't fret like a child because the paint wears off his toys."

They had reached the house, and were stepping through the open window. He broke off with a short laugh, "Heavens! I believe I've been preaching to you. Never mind, the text was a large one, and my homily was as useful as most sermons. Good-night." He shook Fred warmly by the hand and strode off home.

It was next morning that Fred heard from the O'Connors. They presented apologies and compliments; they would be happy to join him on the *Sylph* at twelve o'clock, and might they presume so far as to bring with them their friend Mr. Charles Phillips.

Fred read the note at breakfast. At the first glance he was delighted; at the second he was profoundly embarrassed. He cracked his eggs, munched his toast, and secretly cursed his own want of courage and address.

Kate had awakened radiant. Her passion was like the narrow partial cyclone, which ploughs its way with fierce speed through the fields, tearing everything before it. But on each side of it the sun is shining, the birds are singing, and all is peace. And when its quick course is over the air is still and balmy, and only scattered traces of destruction remain to show that a whirlwind has blown across the land. Kate's anger was cyclonic in its sharp and transient fierceness. She was seldom more winning than when her tears of rage gave place to tears of regret, and both to a sunny smile at once defiant and appealing. In the earlier days of their engagement Fred would mischievously provoke her to wrath just to get the enjoyment of a stormy "tiff," which he knew would end after five minutes in the sweetest of reconciliations. But the pastime had lost its charms for him; and to be perfectly frank, it must be confessed that Kate's whirlwinds came frequently enough to gratify any curiosity without wanton provocation.

This morning she had marched into the breakfast-room with a red rose in her dusky hair and another in her hand. She had gone straight up to Fred, put her hands on his shoulders, and said with a shy audacity, which was bewitching but not convincing, " Freddy, I am very sorry; won't you forgive Kitty's nasty tempers?" Then she kissed him, fastened the rose in his coat, drew him to the table, poured out his coffee—for Mrs. Wynnston breakfasted in bed—and made that display of domestic solicitude which, before marriage, is perhaps the most delicate and irresistible flattery that a woman can offer to the man she loves.

Fred knew that Kate was looking forward with pleasure to their cruise. His cutter had been lying idle in the bay ever since its arrival on the memorable evening of their engagement. He had originally intended to make only a short stay at Lorton, and then to take a month's cruise among the Scotch islands. But many of his intentions had undergone a remarkable change, and he had several times made up his mind to send the *Sylph* back to the seaport from which she hailed, and where she was laid up during the winter. At Kate's suggestion he had arranged for this afternoon sail, but he had not mentioned to her the fact that he had invited the O'Connors to join them.

Now he crumbled his dry toast disconsolately, for he had prevision of a storm. He called himself a fool for asking these people without telling Kate, and wondered how in the world he should get out of his dilemma.

Presently he said uneasily, "I think it will be a fine day."

"Oh yes," said Kate; "I looked at the glass this morning. It has been steady for four-and-twenty hours. We shall have a jolly time, shan't we, Fred?"

That miserable young man rose and looked out of the window. "There's a nice breeze from the south; if it holds we shall have a smart run out and back again."

There was a pause, and presently he went on with a nervous attempt at indifference which a child could have noticed: "By the bye, I told you, Kate, didn't I, that I had asked the O'Connors to join us ? "

The blood leaped to Kate's face and the flush was reflected in his own. " No, you didn't," she replied. " Are they coming ? "

" I've a note here from O'Connor accepting, and asking if he may bring some fellow named Phillips." He tossed the letter across the table to her.

She sprang up, tore the luckless note into fifty pieces and ground them beneath her heel.

" Do you think I'm blind ? " she panted ; " do you think I've been blind all these weeks ? "

" Kate ! Kate ! " he protested, " what in the world do you mean ? "

" Ah ! you never loved as I do, and you think you can befool me. Did I not tell you down there when you asked me to be your wife that you didn't know your own mind? I knew it, though you didn't."

"But, Kitty, I do love you," he feebly interrupted, and drew nearer to her.

She raised her arm as though to thrust him away. "Do I not know the secret of your morning rides? Have I not watched you drifting away from me ever since you came to me? You're tired of me and bored with me, and you've seen some one you think will make you happier. Oh Fred, I love you, I hate you!"

The storm was now over and the gentle rain followed. Kate, sobbing as though her poor little heart would break, fell into her chair and covered her face.

Fred hated scenes. He knew in his inmost soul that there was a good deal of shrewd truth in Kate's passionate outburst. But she was the attacking party; she had flown into a furious rage, a thing he never did, and he began to feel himself a deeply injured person.

He stood before her with his hands in his pockets and began in a tone of priggish virtue: "You're very foolish, Kate, to put yourself into such passions. I suppose you can't help being jealous, but that's no reason why you should behave like this. You've made your eyes all bloodshot, and your face isn't fit to be seen. Such temper must be very bad for you. You really should try to check it."

Kate's hands fell and her eyes blazed again as she looked him in the face.

He went on: "You seem to have no regard or consideration for me. Only yesterday you greatly embarrassed me and shocked Arnitte by your violence. Now to-day you place me

in a most difficult position. I've asked the
O'Connors . to spend the afternoon on the
Sylph—a most ordinary civility—and your
behaviour makes me doubt whether I ought
to go. I don't see how I can stay away,"
—there was a tone of question in his voice,—
"yet it will be most painful for me to go."

A woman's tenderest pity often covers a
vein of scorn. Káte rose and, taking Fred's
hand, said, "I'm very sorry to trouble you
so, Fred; my temper is as great a punishment
to me as it can be to any one else. Of course
you must go. You can't do otherwise."

"When will you be ready?" returned the
young man, grudgingly.

"You must go without me. I've made
myself ill, and, as you say, my face isn't fit
to be seen."

She hastily left the room, and Fred

lighted a cigarette and uneasily paced up and down. Of course he knew he had behaved as meanly as a man could behave, and he was a good deal ashamed of himself. He knew that he ought to send to the O'Connors, and, pleading an accident to the boat or some other reasonable excuse, postpone the expedition. He debated the point with himself, and apparently found it hard to solve, for twelve o'clock drew near and still he was smoking cigarettes and fidgeting up and down. At length he seized his hat and strode with hesitating steps across the lawn down towards the beach.

CHAPTER V

IN the evening the vicar called at Lorton House. Mrs. Wynnston was in distress about her tenors. Basses were plentiful enough, and she had installed half a dozen young fellows in the choir whose trombone-like voices made the old church shake. Balance, she said, was now wanted. They must strengthen the tenors. The tenors indeed needed support. At present they consisted of two mild youths, whose idea of singing tenor was to squeak out on "dominant sevenths" at the end of lines and verses, and to patch up the rest of their parts with

snatches of bass, alto, and soprano. It did
not matter much, for no one could hear them
through the roar of the vigorous and aggres-
sive " basses."   Still, from an artistic point
of view, Mrs. Wynnston was right in de-
manding more tenors.

There was a dearth of them in Lorton.
The vicar had been commissioned by Mrs.
Wynnston to hunt up half a dozen, and he
had been inquiring through the parish for
likely young men. His mission had been
attended with indifferent success. He was
depressed. He was sorely tempted to blas-
pheme all the four parts of harmony.
But Mrs. Wynnston encouraged him. She
pointed out the great necessity of a thorough
reorganisation of the musical portion of the
service. She enlarged upon the attractive-
ness of good singing, held out a tempting

bait of increased offertories, and hinted that respect to Heaven urgently dictated a change from the present slovenly arrangements.

The conversation, or rather the monologue, —for Mrs. Wynnston did most of the talking,—was protracted, and the evening was growing dusk as the vicar stood at the door taking his leave.

"What a glorious evening it is!" he said. "By the way, I haven't seen Kate; where is she to-night?"

"That reminds me," said Mrs. Wynnston, "I wanted to consult you about Kate; our business drove the subject out of my mind. I'm rather concerned about her."

The vicar wakened up to a more obvious interest than he had shown during the "business" discussion. "You alarm me," he said; "is your daughter in ill-health?"

"Oh no; she is well enough. What troubles me is this. You see, she and her cousin have gone and engaged themselves to be married."

"Indeed!" ejaculated the vicar with a long intonation, which expressed surprise, contemplation, and something else not so easy to discover.

Mrs. Wynnston was not quick of apprehension, and without noticing the vicar's interruption went on: "I'm afraid they've been rather hasty. Of course, they're very fond of one another, and I know Kate is devotedly attached to Fred; but for some reason they don't seem to get on very smoothly together. They had a quarrel this morning, I believe, for Kate has been crying in her room all day."

A flush crossed the clear, fresh cheeks of the vicar.

She continued : " Of course, mothers ought
not to interfere in such matters. It never
does any good. It's very difficult to know
what to do. I suppose all will come right
in the end."

"Let us hope so," said the vicar very
gravely. "But I must go now; we will
talk of this another time. Good-night."

He walked out into the dusky lane
plunged deep in meditation. The evening
breeze across the fields stirred with a soothing rustle the thickening ears of corn, and
here and there in playful sport bore down to
his feet from the tree-tops a leaf cut off
before its time. The birds twittered in their
nests, talking together, as it were, of the
adventures and enjoyments of another day.
Far away, below the church, from an old elm
by the brook side, rose up the strong, sweet

song of the nightingale—a musical ecstasy
of sadness.   Above, in the larch woods,
sounded, like an echo of half-spoken fare-
wells, the rich late note of the cuckoo.

But the vicar heard none of these things.
He was saying to himself with a maddening
mechanical iteration, "Little Kate is going to
be married."

He had known her from a child, and had
never seen that she had ceased to be a child.
She had plagued him, mocked him, mimicked
him, and had always been a tender, wayward
little friend.   For ten years her dark eyes
had beamed affectionately on his life.   Then
she was "little Kate," and until half an hour
ago he had never thought of her as anything
but "little Kate."   She was warmly attached
to him.   To the lonely passionate girl he
seemed the only lovable being in Lorton.

She had never known her father, and she loved him as a father. The vicar was lonely too. A hateful woman had chilled his manhood. For years his heart had ached with emptiness, and the child had crept into the void. But he had never known it, never felt it, and now it was surprise which stunned him.

"Oh dear! oh dear! I never dreamed of this," he muttered; and then the old refrain rang again and again in his ears, "Little Kate is going to be married."

His head drooped, and he slowly paced along like one who walks in sleep.

Presently he stopped, clenched his walking-stick tightly, and drew himself up. "This will not do," he said. "What am I thinking; what am I daring to think? Old fool! old parson! you are nearly sixty and— married!"

Married—the sweetest word of happiness, the irrevocable knell of misery. God binds chains of iron round men's lives, but men bind chains of adamant round themselves. The whole living creation craves for union. The flowers mate and bloom; birds, beasts, and men seek and strive for consorts. If conduct is three-fourths of life, love is the other quarter. It keeps life living; it sends spreading and working through the centuries the good and the evil that men do. These are the chains of iron. But there are laws, there are social requirements, there are customs, which men have set up for themselves. By them evil and good are linked together in unbreakable fetters—wise and foolish, grave and frivolous, strong and weak. Hearts that love are severed; hearts that hate are doomed to beat each other to pieces

in enforced contact. These are the chains of
adamant. Conduct is good, conduct is need-
ful, but conduct is hard. Why should life
be made more difficult to live and no more
worth living by social fear and social folly?
Why should men and women be tempted
from small irritations to great sins because of
Hebraic traditions and Philistine prejudices?
There are sins from which no one escapes;
there are griefs which all must endure; there
are weaknesses common to humanity; there are
pains which all must bear. Fate has so ordered
it, and the world must bow. The path of
life at best is rough, yet men seem to walk it
of their own free will in boots that pinch.

Thoughts such as these, wild and bitter,
coursed through the vicar's brain as he strode
on to his home. It was an old house bedded
in richest foliage. The ancient lawns were

soft as velvet. Over the walks old-world gardeners had bent the trees into fifty fantastic arches. Round the grounds ran a high rubble wall, covered within by clinging pear-trees. The house itself—a low, white building—was almost hidden with ivy and with creepers, and the wooden porch blazed with the blossoms of the purple clematis. At the side was a great rose-garden, where the plants stood in rows, as vines grow in a vine-yard. It was the vicar's especial pride. There were thousands of rose-trees, tens of thousands of flowers; the garden gleamed with mingled colours like an artist's palette when his day's work is done. The breeze passing over it came laden with a scent cloying sweet, as is the breath of the Italian fields when the summer moon shines and the white mists rise from the plains.

The house was in darkness, and as he pushed open the door and stood hesitating for a moment within the porch an unwonted sense of solitude stole over him. He was alone in the world. No glow of domestic tenderness brightened the evening of his days. No whisper of peace came from above to comfort him. His faith had long been dead. The past was pain, the present weariness, the future blank. There was nothing but the dark house and the whisper of night among the leaves. The stillness seemed to gather round him and to choke him. He stepped inside and hastily closed the door, then climbed to his observatory, where he was wont to pass silent hours searching the heavens.

It was a small circular room built through the roof. In the middle stood the great telescope, its brass tube glittering like a shaft of ghostly light in the rays of a tiny night-lamp which the vicar carried in his hand. A chronometer on the walls solemnly ticked. On a shelf the spectroscope stretched out its triple limbs. A dozen books stood on a small shelf; one or two celestial charts and a table of logarithms were hanging up. An easy-chair was fixed so that the observer could use the telescope with comfort; and a couple of wheels and a lever enabled the occupant of the chair to direct the telescope, and to turn the entire room round in following the motions of the stars.

This little chamber divided with the rose-garden the vicar's keenest interest and ministered most constantly to his happiness. He would sit for hours peering into the depths of space. His soul would expand

and exult in a sense of limitless and illimit-
able freedom. He would pass in review the
hosts of heaven, would sweep from satellites
to planets, from planets to suns, from suns
to awful congeries faintly glittering on the
threshold of the infinite; then, lost to time
and space, would plunge into misty nebulæ
as the portals through which to seek on the
glowing wings of imagination new galaxies,
new universes.

For many years the vicar had lost all
spiritual emotion, and its place had been
supplied by the physical and intellectual
exaltation produced in him by the scent
and colour of his flowers and by the cold
beauty of the stars. To-night, all troubled
and dismayed, he flung himself down into
his chair to seek peace in the infinite
expanse and eternal calm of space. He

sought but found not. Instead of floating through ether as was his wont, without effort, even the effort of will, he found himself toiling and striving through the unending and everlasting towards a goal which everlastingly receded. The stars maddened him with their fixed stony eyes —he living, panting, struggling, suffering; they lifeless, changeless, cold. He craved for help, for solace, but none came. The stately systems moved round him in their majesty, and as he followed them with yearning look he longed to say to them, "Oh, greater than I, help me and save me!" But the words died upon his lips. "No," he thought, "they are dead; I live and think and suffer. I am better than a whole universe of blind force."

The vicar could bear his loneliness no

longer. Just as he had sought refuge in the house from the sweet stillness of his rose-garden, so now he turned with a groan from his telescope, eager to escape from the unbroken silence of the night. He trimmed his little lamp, took a book, and sat with his elbows on the low shelf where stood his spectroscope, his head resting between his hands. He read of atoms clashing together in the shimmering cloud of nebulous systems, of planets glowing with fervent heat, of whirlwinds of fire, and hail of molten metal, of vapour, of rain, of seas and floods, of earthquakes, of ice, and of great beasts wallowing in the mud of mighty rivers. All passed like a pageant through his mind, but brought no peace. There was no, point in this spectacle of strength and duration on which his human sympathies could fix.

The want was new to him. Formerly he would follow with revelling imagination the path of light flashing through centuries from some far distant sun, or would trace to its creation through ancient fires and floods and glaciers some morsel of stone chipped from the bare hillside. It never had seemed to him that any element of satisfaction or comfort or profit was lacking. Now he was as one who watches a stage with its scenery set for a great drama, where all the appointments are present and all the lights burn, but no player enters and no voice sounds. He ceased to read, and his memory by some unconscious operation called up again the conversation he had with Arnitte over Mrs. Wynnston's dinner-table. "There is no worth or value, intellectual or moral, in a star or its properties apart from the effect produced on human minds." The transcendental mystic had said something of this kind, and had flung at him a tag of Arnold—that knowledge is useless unless correlated with conduct. Well, was not all knowledge inherently worthy? He scribbled logarithms on a slip of white blotting-paper, tried to smile scornfully, and ended by smiling painfully. In his heart he began to doubt whether perfect peace could be drawn down the tube of a telescope, and whether comfort would come at the call of the integral calculus. Then the old jingle came back into his ears, "Little Kate is going to be married."

The dim lamp shone on the vicar's gray hair, and when he raised his head there was conflict, manful strife, showing through his firm set features. This was a weakness which had come on him without warning, all unexpected. It sometimes happens that a man who seems in usual health and spirits learns from his physician that fatal disease has seized him, that the sum of his life must be counted in months, perhaps in weeks. The vicar felt like such a man. He believed himself sound, and suddenly a horror and an agony had fallen upon him. But he would conquer. He was strong; he would fight this thing.

His thoughts were brave, but in spite of his self-reliance his whole being cried out for help and strength. Where should he go? where could he look? He turned over the pages of his book, and at length rose, took his lamp, and went down to his study. A low desk at which he wrote his sermons was in the middle of the room. He placed

the light upon it and strode noiselessly up
and down over the soft thick carpet. Round
him were crowded shelves on which stood
brown volumes of theology and controversy,
the survivals of past years when, as a young
man, with living faith and enthusiasm he
had entered the church, passionately convinced of the truth of what he preached,
and earnestly desirous of winning men to
the knowledge of his Master. Mingled
with these were the classics of his college-
days and works of history, of travel, and
of fiction. He seldom touched them now.
Horace indeed stood on his desk, and by
him Lucretius. In idle moments he would
snatch glimpses of sardonic enjoyment from
the Sybarite, or gain strength and conviction in his materialism from the philosopher. But to find well-fingered works

you had to seek the little shelf in his observatory.

To and fro he paced between the desk and the shelves till a great longing seized him to look for comfort among his forsaken friends. The idea was repugnant to him. It savoured of weakness, of sentimentality. He " pished " to himself, turned his back on the brown rows, and renewed his weary walking and his endless self-searching. At last he took up the little lamp, and, throwing the light forward with outstretched hand, slowly passed along the line of books. Three or four times, with un-certain glance and step, he walked from end to end, and finally pulled out a small old book. Setting down the lamp, he knocked the thick dust from the volume into the fireplace, then seated himself at his desk. Doubt, shame, and hope flitted across his face, and then, as though he had found some expected, half-remembered passage, his finger stayed upon a page.

His lips moved, but no voice sounded as he read, " When a good man is afflicted, tempted, or troubled with evil thoughts, then he understandeth better the great need he hath of God, without whom he perceiveth he can do nothing that is good." He stopped, pondered, and listlessly read on till another passage arrested his attention. "Although thou shouldest possess all created good, yet couldest thou not be happy thereby nor blessed; but in God who created all things consisteth thy whole blessedness and felicity."

He leaned back in his chair, his hands fell into his lap. The draught from an open window blew over and over the leaves of the book. An old chord had been sounded in the

vicar's heart, a long dammed-up spring of
memory had been set free. He was young
again, with life before him, with faith and with
love in his nature. Both had failed him. His
reason had rejected the dogmas of his childhood, and the woman upon whom all the
tenderness of his youth was poured had filled
his life with misery. The remembrance was
bitter, but it was good. Long he sat there
motionless, thinking, thinking, thinking. And
as he thought a barrier as of ice between him
and his soul slowly melted away. The light
of morning, gray and cold, showed through
the window's " glimmering square," and the
vicar's eyes were full, and tears were trickling
down his face.

He bent forward once more and read, " O
Lord my God, be not Thou far from me ; my
God, have regard to help me ; for there have

risen up against me sundry thoughts and great fears afflicting my soul."

Gently he closed the book, went to his bed, and slept.

Another trial was before him. The morning was Sunday, and the vicar rose tranquil and composed. He breakfasted and glanced over the notes of an old sermon, for he had no inclination to prepare a fresh one, jotted down in pencil one or two new points, and then, as an hour remained before church time, strolled out into his rose-garden. He drank in the fresh air, the sweet scents, and the bright colours, with something of his old exhilaration. He had a secret sense of shame at his last night's agitation.

The experience is not a singular one. How many of us have composed eloquent speeches, written scenes of heartrending pathos, or come

to heroic resolutions overnight, and blushed
to remember it in the morning. A cruel spirit
of common sense pervades the early hours;
the morning light is remorselessly searching.
Nocturnal eloquence then seems absurd;
pathos becomes bathos—heroism, imbecility.

The vicar struck his stick upon the gravel
paths, squared his yet straight and broad
shoulders, and inwardly desired to pick up
St. Thomas à Kempis, still lying on the desk,
and push him to the back of the dusty shelves.
Possibly he would have done it had not a
creaking gate in the wall swung open, and
Kate Wynnston hurriedly tripped along the
path towards him.

There was nothing unusual in her visit.
She was "free" of the rose-garden, a privilege
only enjoyed by the vicar's first favourites.
She would come in at all times, would revel

after her sensuous manner among the flowers, would wage deadly war upon certain little green flies which grew fat in opening buds and curling leaves, would deck her hair with the choicest blossoms. There were many roses in Mrs. Wynnston's garden, but they never seemed so fragrant to Kate as her "dear old vicar's." Often she would burst in upon him on Sunday mornings before church, merrily threaten him with Mrs. Wynnston's newest scheme of church reform, walk across the churchyard with him, and perhaps take her place along with his old housekeeper in his square pew below the "three-decker" pulpit.

He was always glad to see her bright face, but this morning his first impulse was to hasten to the house and shut the door. He obeyed the second, which was to swing round and meet her. She came with both hands

extended, and, as he took them in his, he
noticed that her eyes were sunken and heavy,
and that her lip quivered a little. They
turned towards the house. What the vicar
said he never could remember; perhaps it was
some comment on the weather or the roses.
But in his heart he was repeating, " Help me,
for there have risen up against me sundry
thoughts and great fears afflicting my soul."

There was a silence which Kate broke.

" I—I want to speak to you," she said ;
"please will you help me if you can, and tell
me what to do."

They seated themselves, the vicar on a
garden-seat with an elm trunk for the back,
she on a log at his feet. They often sat there
" watching," as Kate said, " the roses grow."

" Forgive me for troubling you," she continued ; "perhaps I ought not to talk even

to you. I don't know. I have nobody in all the world to go to; and oh! I am so very, very unhappy."

There was a dry despair in her voice more painful than tears. The vicar laid his hand upon her head and caressed her dark curls.

"It's Fred, my cousin," she said, as though the vicar needed no further explanation. "He was so good to me when I was little—better than anybody else; we always said we should be married; and once, when we were very little, we ran away together. I've always loved him" (this very softly). "I never could love anybody else in this world; and now" (with a tearless sob) "he is tired of me. I've driven him away with my temper and jealousy, and he has seen some one he likes better. What shall I do? what shall I do?"

Kate could not see the vicar's face, or she

would have forgotten her own troubles. He
was youthful for his years, and few lines of
care and age had marked his features. Just
now he looked a hundred. Several times he
tried to speak, but the words died away in
his throat.   Kate must have felt the trembling of his hand upon her head.

At length he said, " Poor little lassie !
Everything seems very dreary, doesn't it, and
life hard to bear, and hope all gone ? Yet,
my dear, you have not begun to know trouble.
In the spring there are cold, rough days when
the wind blows and the hail beats, but next
morning the sun shines, and the world is
bright and warm. And then summer lies
ahead, and every week brings fewer storms
and more leaves and buds. Such weather is
easily borne. It is when the leaves are falling, and the nights bring frost, and the earth

grows harder, and the green things have gone, and winter and darkness are before, that storms are really searching. Do you understand me, Kate?"

"I think," she said, "the storm in spring is worst, for then we have a right to expect sunshine."

"And there *is* sunshine, my little spring flower," he replied, "and there will be sunshine, and the summer must follow. I do not say your griefs are light, girl, but, believe me, no grief is mortal till the autumn has come, till life's tree has ceased to shoot, till life's course is unalterably fixed. Cheer up, lassie, and be sure that whatever happens now these clouds must pass away, for your summer has not begun. Think of those for whom there is never more summer, and be comforted."

She thought he spoke of his own short

and ruined season of happiness, and she took his hand and pressed it between hers. He bent forward and kissed her forehead.

"We must go to church now," he said; "it is time."

Kate sat in the square pew beneath him and greatly wondered as he read the service. He was never in earnest before, and never seemed in earnest. Now his whole nature quivered with fervour. The bumpkins around saw and heard nothing new or strange. Kate vibrated in sympathy with the poor unloved parson. Who has not felt that splendid crescendo of entreaty with which the Litany closes? Prayer upon prayer has floated upward in the calm devout tones of the priest, and the people have whispered their beseechings. Then yearning grows and prayer becomes passion; the voices quicken, and at last people and priest together besiege the throne of God: "Lamb of God, that takest away the sins of the world, have mercy upon us." "Lord, have mercy upon us." "Christ, have mercy upon us."

As he read his tones rose and rang above the dull rustic voices, and the anguish of them struck one hearer with pity and amazement. Then the passion was assuaged, and in quiet reverence the Lord's Prayer should have fallen from the lips of the priest. But for a moment he was silent, bent forward on his knees. The vicar was praying.

Praying! Yes, but to whom? Was it to an all-strong, all-good Being watching from afar over the petty lives and fates of men, ready to bestow help and comfort upon those who ask? Or was the man appealing to all that was best and truest in himself, drawing from fountains of strength hidden deep in his own nature? Who can tell? Perhaps he was not sure himself.

Enough to know that the vicar's prayer was answered.

CHAPTER VI

THE war was followed by a truce.

Fred, somewhat ashamed of himself, and really concerned by the obvious grief of his cousin, grew kindly and even tender. The vicar found an opportunity of speaking to him, in the most delicate and affectionate way, of his duty to Kate and of the great trouble she was experiencing.

Fred would have resented this interference if he had found a chance. But the vicar was too clever a man of the world to give him one, and besides, Fred could not but recognise his right, as Mrs. Wynnston's nearest male friend, to act in the matter. The conversation was quite casual in outward forms and hypothetical in its terms. But Fred recognised its legitimate application, and at its close shook the vicar's hand with the most friendly goodwill and respect.

Kate, for her part, was much gentler and more patient. She could not forget the vicar's words in the garden and his tones in the pulpit. She did not understand his deep anguish, but she knew it existed, and her own troubles seemed to grow trivial before it.

A woman's life is to be glad and to be sorry. Good women rarely know what agony of soul is. Perhaps they do not know joy of soul either. Hand in hand with a lover, or chirruping to a first-born child, a woman is happy with a happiness as bright as the blitheness of a bird. The lover proves false, the child dies, and see her tears, her wringing of hands, listen to her cries of pain. The trouble seems very real, and so it is to her. But the cure is usually certain, often speedy. Sometimes there is balsam in a black bonnet. What would you? For her the hidden things of life do not exist. It is not her fault, but the fault of social conventions which mould her nature. She has learned that her functions are to love, to marry, to bear children, to dress becomingly, to go to church, to curtsey in the creed to the Second Person of the Trinity, to play the piano, to read the last novel, perhaps to dance and to make pastry. She goes through life smiling and crying. Not for her are agonies of doubt, searchings of spirit, high endeavour, divine renunciation. Woman, indeed, is the sacrifice of man, only she does not know it, and a sacrifice made unconsciously is no sacrifice. She bears the limitations of her existence as she bears her children, patient in pain and peril, believing that she fulfils her duty. It is pitiful, not heroic. When our first parents robbed the tree of knowledge, Eve but tasted the fruit, Adam alone ate it to the core. Yet there are women whose eyes have been opened, who have peered into the heart of earth's mystery, who have drunk deep the sweet and bitter draughts of life. And what are they? where are they found? Look at their haggard faces, hear their hollow laughter, seek them in dark corners. Shameless and unsexed you call them; so some are, but not all. Have you thrilled from head to foot when that great actress as Cleopatra, clasping her dying lover to her bosom, cries, with

an agony that stops the beating of your
heart—

> "Die where thou hast lived;
> Quicken with kissing; had my lips that power,
> Thus would I wear them out."

A school-girl could not have done it. Nor
could your good-wife, who, sitting a little
shamefaced at your side, whispers, "How
very pathetic!" You are glad that she
could not, and perhaps you are right. That
actress has felt the surge of passion. She is
only kissing a paid player to whom she will
carelessly nod as she passes him to-morrow.
See how her breast heaves, the blood mounts
to her face, she strains the body of her
Antony closer and closer, her voice is choked
in one long kiss. It is only acting. Ah!
but how did she learn to do it? The world
applauds and admires the actress. In the
life of the woman there are passages which

men discuss with many a brutal jest, which
women whisper amid the clatter of the teacups, and nod and wag their heads. If your
wife met her in the street she would gather
up her skirts. You are rather pleased; you
would be shocked if your wife clasped her
hand, kissed her polluted lips, and said, "Poor
sister."   Don't fear.   There is no danger.
Your estimable spouse is incapable of such a
breach of decorum.

Mrs. Wynnston having settled the great
tenor question more or less satisfactorily,
found time to devote some attention to Kate's
affairs.   She did not understand her daughter,
and even Fred's simpler character perplexed
her.   She reasoned with herself—"Here are
two young people, good-looking, comfortable
in circumstances, fond of one another, companions from childhood, evidently destined

by fortune for one another; why should they not make love and get married like sensible beings, instead of squabbling and sulking and making themselves miserable? In my time boys and girls were made more reasonable. What is coming to the rising generation I don't know. What can a body do with two such stupid lovers? If I sympathise with Kate she will fly at me; if I remonstrate with Fred he will think Kate has complained to me and go into the sulks for a´week. Perhaps I had better leave them alone, yet I feel it's my duty to do something. If I only knew what."

She ended by writing to Mr. Hazzleden, senior.

Three or four mornings after Fred found the following letter by his plate at breakfast:—

"My dear Boy—What have you been doing with yourself all these weeks? It is quite a month since you wrote to me. I thought you were cruising among the Hebrides, or gone in search of the North Pole, and now I infer from that wonderful woman, your Aunt Wynnston, who sends me a beautiful letter three times a year, that you are still at Lorton. What is the reason of it? From your aunt's account I should imagine you had joined the church choir and were singing tenor all day and a considerable portion of the night. I admire your aunt, Fred, but her letters are a little confusing. Or is it black-eyed Kitty who has kept you? Now don't write 'yes' or I'll disinherit you. I tell you I'm jealous. I never think with patience of that bit in the prayer-book about a man not marrying his niece. The old buffers who wrote it couldn't have been uncles. Anyhow, they hadn't Kitty Wynnston for a niece. I only wish she was here. That good soul, your Aunt Maria, will drive me crazy. She's a 'hyper-Calvinist' now, she says. I don't quite know what that is; do you? It's something unpleasant, for yesterday I just read her a chapter of Darwin (I do wish you would read Darwin, Fred, the greatest man of the century), and your worthy Aunt Maria said it was all very fine, but she was content to know she was preordained to salvation, and I was preordained to another 'ation.' It's very consoling for her, no doubt, but I say it's all confounded nonsense. There are some new people, by the way, in Dr. Gordon's old house. I suppose it belongs to Miss O'Connor now. The man is called Williamson, was something 'in shoes,' made money, shaky on h's, and rather fat. Your Aunt Maria and Mrs. W. have struck up an acquaintanceship. She is an inoffensive woman, young for her years, and as amiable as she is ungrammatical. She too has a turn for theology, and your aunt and she make the evenings hideous with their eternal chatter. Your aunt confided to me that Mrs. W. was 'a poor creature clothed in the filthy rags of righteousness and preordained to perdition from before the foundation of the world.' I suppose Maria knows, for she has gone deeply into the subject; but upon my word, Fred, I think it was anything but kind of Providence to do such wholesale preordination and not give men and women a chance. I ventured to suggest this idea to your aunt, but I was sorry afterwards. She went off into a sermon on free will. She said my doubts were all the result of my stubborn belief in free will. She wanted no free will; she knew where her free will would lead her,—'Free grace if you like, John, but no free will.' I certainly have noticed that your aunt has abundance of will; as she says it is not 'free,' I suppose it isn't. Darwin, my boy, is a great help in all this nonsense. He never wastes his time over such stuff. That retired boot-man, W., is frightfully ignorant. I just sounded him the other day as to his views on the origin of species, and he did not seem to have any very definite opinions. So I asked him what he thought of Darwin. He said he didn't know much about it himself, but he knew a man who had a mill there. The idiot thought I meant some wretched town where they make cotton or something. We have a new curate here, a dear young creature, whom your aunt immediately pre-ordained to a place with the patriarchs. I've lent him 'Natural Selection,' but I don't expect it will do him much good. It's very hard to drive sense into the head of a parson. I was only arguing evolution with him yesterday. He pretended that he could never see any possible link between vegetable and animal life. I took him into the vinery, Fred. Any man who has grown vines must know that plants aren't half such fools as they look. The vines, as you know, run along the roof. One of them has a branch hanging a foot from the glass. Six inches above it a wire runs all along. Would you believe it, in a fortnight that vine had shot up half a dozen tendrils, hooked them over the wire, and the branch is now hanging as safely and comfortably as possible. I pointed this out to our curate, and he screwed up his eyes and said something about the beautiful designs of Providence. All bosh, Fred, and I told him so. That vine has what Darwin calls a low form of consciousness—just the same consciousness as yours and mine, only less of it. If this is so, where is the difficulty of the evolution of men from plants, the lower forms giving place to the higher? For my part I should not be the least ashamed to trace my ancestry to a cabbage. Indeed, I've noticed manifestations of practical common - sense about several species of cabbages which would really surprise you. But I must tell you all about that another time, for I am gossiping on and quite forgetting the chief reason of my letter. Last week I ran up to town and breakfasted with one of the 'Whips.' He tells me the dissolution cannot be delayed more than a few weeks. The Government really is in a minority, and a vote of censure may be carried almost any night. The Premier has made up his mind not to resign, so an appeal to the country must be taken. The Whip was good enough to say he knew a seat which would just suit you, where you will have to fight, but with an excellent chance of winning. I think you had better come home to-morrow or the day after, when we can talk the matter over. The Whip expressed his great surprise that I, a high and dry old Tory, should be anxious to see my son a Liberal candidate. To be quite frank, Fred, I am delighted that in this respect, at any rate, you are a better man

than your father. You see, your sainted
mother had Conservative tendencies, and I
am a peaceful person. Has Kate any politics?
Ordinary girls call themselves Tories; they
think it more respectable. But Kate isn't
an ordinary girl. Bless her bonny face, I
warrant she's a Republican, or something
equally dreadful. I remember once when
she was a little chit she refused to kneel
down to say her prayers. Her mother
punished her, and, of course, it was very
naughty, but I gave her a penny. Don't
tell your aunt or my character will be gone
for ever. I always think that Darwin
throws a strong light on party politics. You
see, there are two ways of looking at the
world. One is that it was made in six
separate pieces, and that the whole job was
completed when Adam lost that rib of his.

The other is that it slowly grew through millions of years, that it is not finished yet, that it is always developing and is always capable of development. The first is the Tory view. We think things are very good as they are, always were as good as they could be, and that it is our duty to do nothing in particular. The other is the Liberal view. You think that new forms, new thoughts, new methods are always being evolved; that in society the less complex is always giving birth to the more complex; that it is your duty to promote the process in every way you can. We have an ideal behind us, you have one before you. Perhaps you don't quite know what it is, and what it is worth. Still you are always trying to get at it by steps of natural and artificial selection. After all this you will

say I am a queer sort of Tory. I often think
I am; yet I tell you, Fred, if I had a vote
in your constituency I would give it against
you. Ever since I married I have voted
Tory, and I'm too old to change now. If
I voted Liberal even for you, your poor
mother would not rest in peace. Now, just
one serious word. I have always hoped that
you would some day marry my little pet.
If you and she have arranged it I am very
glad. If not, I only wish she may get as
good a husband as I know my lad would
make. But you must be prudent. You
want to go into Parliament, and I should
like to see you there. It is one thing to
be a member as a bachelor and another as a
married man. We have not a great deal
of money, and when I am gone I expect
you will have to give up this place and settle

entirely in town. So, my dear boy, think
over all these things before you make up
your mind. You must remember Kate as
well as yourself *   *   *   *. That
man Williamson has just been here. It
seems he took his girls last week to see some
actor give a drawing-room entertainment.
Mrs. W. has strong views about theatrical
amusements and remonstrated. W. defended himself and came to get my opinion
in the matter. 'I told Jane,' he said, 'the
man hadn't his play-hactin' clothes on, and
that makes all the difference. Don't you
think it does?' I said the point was a
very nice one, but I thought that he had
very accurately discriminated between legitimate and illegitimate theatricals. He has
gone away quite happy. Give my love to
your aunt and Kate, and with the same to

yourself, I am, my dear Fred, your affectionate father, JOHN HAZZLEDEN.

"*P.S.*—I have spent the whole day in writing this and must run off to water the greenhouse. I promised to read a chapter of 'Darwin on Worms' to your Aunt Maria to-night, but I'm afraid there won't be time."

Fred packed his bag and asked Arnitte to stay with him a few days at home, and afterwards give him a lift with his election business. Next day the pair started for Mr. Hazzleden's house.

CHAPTER VII

SOUTH the travellers journeyed to Barkleigh
Junction, a great railway centre named from
the village of Barkleigh, and ten miles
from Soarceter, a thriving and populous
manufacturing town. Mr. Hazzleden lived a
couple of miles from Barkleigh, and when he
succeeded to his father's property thirty-five
years ago Soarceter was a quaint old place,
consisting principally of coaching inns and
churches, and remarkable for nothing except
some Roman remains, which the people would
tell you were built by Julius Cæsar, who was
Pope of Rome many years ago, and who took

a great number of Englishmen prisoners in battle, and set them free again because they looked like angels. This tradition is supposed to lack historical foundation, but the people of Soarceter a generation back lived and died believing it. They were moderately happy and prosperous in their lives, and their descendants are firmly convinced that they ultimately achieved perpetual felicity. If so, what reason have we for boasting? We have reached a high degree of culture, we know that Cæsar was not Pope, that he crossed the Rubicon, and that Brutus killed him i' the Capitol. Yet the old Soarceter folk earned their bread with a little butter, and at last went to heaven. At length a remarkable change came over the spirit of Soarceter life. A persevering cobbler in a cellar in the High Street discovered a new and cheaper way of making boots. For a few years he kept his discovery to himself, but when he left his cellar and went into the biggest shop in the town the secret leaked out. The people of Soarceter seemed at once to be inspired by the genius of bootmaking. They worked in " soles " and " uppers " as poets work in words and thoughts. They were born cobblers, not made. They revelled in their calling, perfected its smallest details, and scraped together comfortable fortunes. The cellars gave place to shops, the shops to big factories. Every one prospered. The factory hands saved money and eventually became, employers themselves. Five times over the population doubled itself, and Soarceter became one of the great towns of England.

Mr. Hazzleden watched this growth with interest. Many of his friends became very rich on the prosperity of Soarceter. They bought up land in the town when land was worth little, and sold it again when the industry of a hundred struggling bootmakers had made it worth so much that if you had covered it with a carpet of £5 notes you would have hardly exceeded its market value. Mr. Hazzleden had never increased his means by speculating upon the success of his fellows. He did not like the principle. " I don't make boots myself," he said, "and I don't see why I should put my hand in the pockets of the man who does." Mr. Hazzleden drew his income from his farm land and his consols, and remained comparatively poor. His friends and the world generally said, "Serve him right." Soarceter had been a gold mine to the industrious and the idle alike, and the man who refused to dig for nuggets, and who declined to permit other people to pour them into his lap, deserved to be hard up.

Mr. Hazzleden scorned the pity of his acquaintances as much as he scorned their means of making money. He watched them heap investment upon investment and then disappear—for Barkleigh presented few attractions to the affluent. He himself was happy enough. His only regret was that Soarceter had spread over the hilltop, that a cluster of distant factory chimneys was visible from the dining-room windows, and that the west wind was sometimes laden with more smoke than was good for the flowers and fruit. Accident, and to some extent disposition, made him a solitary man. His wife died when he was still young, and he never married again. The growth of

Soarceter dispersed all gentle society in which he might have found intimate acquaintances. Walking through the old Soarceter market-place he sometimes pointed out to Fred the occupants of the splendid carriages which dashed about. "See that man," he would say, as a pompous old fellow clattered past; "twenty years ago he sold pies from a tray in this very market-place. I remember when you were a little lad you used to tease your mother for coppers to buy his cakes. He was mayor last year and entertained the Prince of Wales. He expeets to be knighted." Again he would remark, "Look at that handsome woman with the red parasol, the one behind the green livery. You see her? She was our first cook at Barkleigh, before you were born. She married a factory hand who invented a new loop for pulling on boots, and I suppose she's worth a hundred thousand pounds at least. Her husband has been dead several years, and I'm afraid there's some truth in the scandal which has been talked of her."

So he reviewed the mushroom magnificence of Soarceter. He was not envious or contemptuous of it. His own equals and companions had been enriched and driven away by it, but he owed it no grudge. He felt the enormous advantage which a community possesses where the poorest members may hope to raise themselves to comfort and wealth by industry and ingenuity. Mr. Hazzleden was not a man of high education. He was a country gentleman, the son of a country gentleman, bred in the tradition that it is a much finer thing to take a five-bar gate neatly, and to shoot straight, than to read Homer, Virgil, or Milton. But he was of singularly powerful mind, and looked at all questions from a high, clear standpoint. He felt his own limitations and regretted them, and his son Fred he sent to Rugby and Oxford. Of course he could not emancipate himself entirely from the prejudices of his class. That would have been superhuman. He always refused the hospitality of the pieman mayor, and shunned those social circles where his ancient cook was a great lady. Maybe it was weakness, but it was natural.

Mr. Hazzleden's dogcart awaited the arrival of Fred and Arnitte at the station. Fred took the reins, Arnitte mounted beside him. They drove past a dozen red brick villas, very new, very respectable, and bearing an indescribable appearance of awkward and unaccustomed

affluence.   As they turned up the lane to
Barkleigh Fred heaved a sigh of relief, and
said, "Now we're out of the atmosphere of
boots."

"You don't like the smell of leather," returned Arnitte.   "Ah, but if you want to get
into Parliament you must learn to relish worse
smells."

"I don't mind leather," said Fred; "it's
brass which smells so nasty.   I wonder how it
is that a rich boor is so much more offensive
than a poor one.   You can tolerate beneath
corduroy what is insufferable beneath broad-
cloth.   The people about here by industry and
skill have made money, yet they are much less
to my taste than the men who are still earning
a pound a week."

Arnitte laughed.   "Your Radicalism is as
remarkable as what you tell me of your father's

Toryism. My dear boy, your stiff-neckedness will some day get you into trouble. I shouldn't be surprised if you so far forgot yourself as to shake hands with a duke."

It was Fred's turn to laugh now. "Upon my word, Arnitte," he said, "you can call a fellow a snob as neatly as any one I know. What I said sounded snobbish, I dare say, but it wasn't meant so. I detest men whose pockets are always bulged out, who seem always to be saying, 'I began life as an errand boy, and now I'm worth £10,000 a year.' Surely it isn't always snobbish to despise the upstart who has lived to make money?"

"Yet," returned Arnitte, "I think it can be argued that money is the only thing worth living for."

"Perhaps it can, but you are the last man to do it," Fred warmly replied, for he was no believer in the genuineness of his friend's cynicism.

"Don't be so sure of that. Remember what your Political Economy handbook tells you— 'Money is not wealth.' To suppose that it is involves a moral as well as an economic fallacy. The man who lives merely to get wealth is a beast, but I don't think every eager money-getter is. You are going to say I am chopping straws." Arnitte had an irritating trick of anticipating his opponent's retorts in argument; he was a thought-reader.

Fred nodded; he knew his friend's unconscious habit.

"It's not straw-chopping," Arnitte went on. "Money is the greatest instrument of enlightenment and civilisation in the world, and those who have none ought to live to get as much as they honestly can. Look at the

VII FREDERICK HAZZLEDEN

people in those hideous villas. When they
were children they probably lived in ugly
squalid houses, grinding ten hours a day to
make a few shillings, and finding no pleasure
in life but beer and tobacco. Now they live
in comfort and in some degree of refinement.
The man perhaps buys pictures. He has no
more taste than a Hottentot; still it's a sign
of grace that he cares to have pictures on his
walls. His wife is dreadfully vulgar in her
silk gowns and jewels, but I believe she is a
more civilised creature than when she was a
slipshod factory hand finding no shame in her
dirty cotton rags. The bumptious vulgarity
of the pair offends you. But what can you
expect? Social refinement only comes with
breeding. You're not compelled to make
them your bosom friends. On the other
hand, you shouldn't despise them because

they've made money and are proud of it."

Fred meditatively flicked the horse with his whip, and presently replied, "There's a good deal of truth in what you say. I tell you what it is," he went on, "it's a pity you're not going to try for Parliament instead of me. We want men with ideas there. You have plenty; I've none."

Arnitte shrugged his shoulders. "I may have some ideas," he said, "but I have no idea of going into your Parliament."

The pronoun and the slight accent which he laid upon it struck Fred as peculiar. Then the Parliament was not his Parliament. Fred remembered a discussion he had had with Kate a few weeks before. Kate declared that Arnitte was not an Englishman. Fred, on the other hand, was of opinion that no foreigner could be so thoroughly acquainted with English affairs and so perfectly at home in English society. As a matter of fact neither of them could remember to have heard him refer in any way to his past life. Who he was, where he came from, and what had brought him to Lorton were mysteries. They could only agree that he was a gentleman, an accomplished man, and a very delightful companion.

When they reached Mr. Hazzleden's door, Fred jumped down to greet his father, who came out to welcome them.

"Well, Fred, my boy, how are you? Mr. Arnitte, glad to see you, sir. I've heard of you from my sister-in-law, Mrs. Wynnston," and he shook his guest warmly by the hand. "Mrs. Wynnston thinks there's something supernatural about you. She told me all you'd

done.   Now, Darwin's a great help in these
matters.   All natural enough.   You're a fine
example of evolution, sir."

Arnitte knew from Fred of his father's
hobby, and gravely replied that he too had
found Darwin of great assistance in many
difficulties.

Mr. Hazzleden stopped to shake Arnitte's
hand once more.   " I'm delighted to see you,
sir—delighted.   You've read him, and of course
you've found him a help.   The greatest man
of the century, sir.   But we'll have a long
talk after dinner.   There are several points
on which I should like to have your opinion."

Fred followed Arnitte into his room.
" Dear old dad," he said, " I'm sure you'll like
him.   Don't think he's a fool because he's
Darwin mad, for he's one of the shrewdest and
most observant men I ever knew."

Arnitte made some kindly reply.

"Ring if you want anything. We dine at six, and the first bell has just gone." Fred went off to his own room.

A party of four sat down to dinner. There were Mr. Hazzleden, Aunt Maria, Fred, and Arnitte. The last quietly noted his surroundings. It was an old-fashioned room with three large windows. Two of them looked out over flower-beds and a small lawn up to an orchard. Seen out of the other a stretch of cornfields, broken only by the red roofs of Barkleigh cottages, extended to the distant chimneys of Soarceter, a vanguard advancing over the hill. The furniture was old and something the worse for wear. A mahogany easy-chair upholstered in some velvet-like material of crimson colour stood by the hearth-rug. On the back was a dark-patch where evidently for many years Mr. Hazzleden's head had rested, as in the evening after early supper he pored over the pages of Darwin, and perhaps read a passage aloud to Aunt Maria knitting stockings on the other side of the fireplace. In a shallow alcove stood a sideboard with a tall looking-glass back. On it were a dozen quaint pieces of china. At each side, on a crochet mat of red wool, was a round ball of china, deep blue in colour, with clouded markings. There were three or four small teacups, some cracked, also a flask-shaped object, which reminded one of a powder-flask in blue china. Three large vases stood at the back, very old and valuable, and the middle one bore a great mass of bright flowers. There were flowers every-where—on the sideboard, on the table, on brackets on the walls. Some, especially the pansies, were most unusual in shape and colour. Mr. Hazzleden, who was very proud of them, called Arnitte's attention to them.

" Governor's own breeding," ejaculated Fred with a twinkle.

Arnitte looked inquiringly.

" Get up early in the morning and you'll find him in the pansy-bed with a camel's-hair brush impiously interfering with the order of nature."

Mr. Hazzleden laughed and explained that by transferring the pollen from one flower to another with a small brush it was possible to blend shapes and colours in a very remarkable manner. He had been most successful in this method—thanks to Darwin, he said, from whom he had gleaned many hints as to the principles of selection. Mr. Hazzleden was now fairly launched upon a favourite

topic. He broached the theory of the consciousness of plants and gave a dozen illustrations in support of it. He was plucking
a large double fuchsia that morning when
his nail slipped and he accidentally inflicted
a long jagged wound on the stalk. " I was
sorry," he said, " because I hate cruelty."

" But surely you don't suppose," interrupted Arnitte, " that the plant was hurt,
that it felt any pain ?"

" Precisely what I do suppose, my dear sir,"
replied Mr. Hazzleden. " Depend upon it,
that fuschia is suffering from my carelessness.
Now, if I scratched you perhaps you would
jump and cry out. Plants can't do that;
their feelings are slower. But if you saw
that fuschia now, if you noticed how it has
drawn up and contracted its wounded limb,
how listlessly the leaves hang near the

wound, you would believe that the plant was suffering."

He went on with great earnestness, explaining his theories of vegetable life. Plants had some rudimentary social sense, he said. Put two flowers side by side in the greenhouse and both would languish; move them apart and both would thrive. Some people were greatly perplexed to explain these facts. To him they were simple enough. When a man and woman of uncongenial dispositions married they soon became unhappy. Now, plants had their sympathies and antipathies just like human beings. Condemn two antipathetic plants to companionship and they began to pine, and if not separated at length died. In answer to a question from Arnitte he declared that he had not been able to imagine how and through what medium plants formed their impressions and received their sensations. Of course they had neither eyes, noses, nor ears like human beings, yet he felt sure they had some sensations corresponding to sight and smell, if not to hearing also. "This should be no difficulty to you at any rate, Mr. Arnitte, for you can see into men's minds with your eyes shut."

Arnitte was interested and amused. In spite of the apparent extravagance of his host's theories he was not disposed to assert that there was no element of truth in them. And then Mr. Hazzleden had such a wide knowledge of plants, and for years had employed such acute powers of observation, that he could give plausible evidence in support of all his propositions. Arnitte mentally decided that Fred was right in regarding his father as an unusually shrewd and observant man.

From the foot of the table Aunt Maria talked to Fred. She was a little, thin-faced woman of sixty, with a long, sharp nose, straight lips and high-arched eyebrows, which made her always appear as though she had just thought something very astonishing. Inward surprise was her constant expression. In this respect, however, her face was deceptive. Aunt Maria was too much engaged in the contemplation of those celestial duties and delights to which she believed she was preordained, to wonder greatly at any mere mundane matters. In truth, she was a kind-hearted old maid who cheerfully occupied her hands with the domestic concerns of Mr. Hazzleden's house while her mind was revelling among the golden streets of the New Jerusalem. But for an occasional touch of rheumatism she might have imagined herself bodily there.

At such times she would rub the afflicted
part with a decoction of her own manufacture
and earnestly murmur, "Ah, there'll be no
pain there." What with the lotion and what
with the thought, Aunt Maria contrived to
endure her aching, and even to extract some
subtle enjoyment from it. She was a rather
provoking controversialist. From incessant
brooding, matters of faith had assumed a
concrete reality in her mind which admitted
of no discussion. It seemed foolish to dispute whether there was such a place as
Heaven when Aunt Maria could give you
the carats of the golden pavement and the
tide times of the Jasper Sea. She was
equally well acquainted with the duties of
the future life and the services required to
attain it. In all these matters she was
placidly certain, and would no more doubt

the reality and truth of her convictions than she would doubt that King John signed Magna Charta, or that Paris is the capital of France. She was not self-righteous or uplifted; she simply regarded her preordination as a divine mystery to be accepted without question. It did not confer upon her any sense of personal superiority. She was a humble little woman, who, in spite of her grotesque creed, lived a useful, self-sacrificing life. She was full of pity and charity to all mankind, except indeed the Jesuits, whom she regarded as incarnations of the evil one, and whose handiwork she saw in every crime committed in the country. For those who differed from her she had a gentle toleration which was sometimes rather irritating. Fred, out of mischief, would argue with her such momentous questions as whether the saints are now in the enjoyment of full bliss or awaiting in a middle sphere the final aecomplishment of the prophecies, or whether the service of Heaven is all praise, or praise and prayer combined. This latter was a favourite topic of Aunt Maria. She held strong views upon it, and defended them with a dexterity and a knowledge of the Scriptures bearing on the problem which were most formidable. "No prayer, Fred," she once said, "no prayer. It's all praise there." Fred, with the levity of youth, expressed some heterodox opinion, but Aunt Maria was not ˙shocked. She had too much confidence in her religious convictions. She knew that he was preordained to salvation, and his theological eecentricities gave her no trouble. Every argument she closed with " Ah, my dear boy, you'll know some day," and then she smiled, nodded, twiddled her thumbs, perhaps dropped a tear, and sat silently staring into that eternity which had become as familiar to her as church on Sunday. There was no shaking her serene confidence. Sometimes, when she had lightly brushed aside the dicta of Darwin, Mr. Hazzleden impatiently retorted, "Maria, you know nothing about it. You never read him, and I can't make you understand his first principles." Then the dear old thing, forgetting her sixty years, answered, "Out of the mouth of babes and sucklings, John, out of the mouth of babes and sucklings; ah! you'll know some day." A part of the future great reward for which Aunt Maria looked was, evidently, the confusion of those who encountered her in argument. Whatever doubts may rest on her creed, none can be cast upon her fidelity to duty.   She managed Mr. Hazzleden's house with firmness and skill, and exerted a controlling influence felt in every corner of it. Mr. Hazzleden often said in simple admiration, "Maria, it's a pity you never got married.   You'd have made a splendid wife." Then she would sigh, perhaps simper, and say, "Who knows, John, maybe it's all for the best." When a young girl Maria had been engaged to a curate.   He jilted her, and the affection which she bestowed on the individual seemed to spread over the whole class.   She had a weakness for curates; she subscribed to their benevolent societies and made them slippers.   In her heart, it is probable, she still cherished a faint, tender hope of making happy the home of some parson. Old maids have a curious power of self-deception; the older they get the bigger does the possibility of marriage loom in their minds. The handsome woman of forty, when rallied by some intimate friend on her single- ness, will laughingly reply that she is too old and ugly to find a husband. When the same woman is fifty-five the same jest will call up a flush of self-consciousness and a dis- ingenuous answer that she "doesn't want to get married." The explanation seems to be that so long as marriage is quite within the bounds of probability, a woman regards her future with easy indifference ; but as soon as age has put it out of the question her thoughts brood on matrimonial companion- ship with morbid intensity, and she begins to persuade herself that more unlikely things have happened than that she should find a husband. Thus it occurred that Aunt Maria, if not absorbed in devotional meditation, treated with an attention almost coquettish any young men, especially curates, who visited Mr. Hazzleden's house.

It was not until dinner was over, and the three men were smoking their cigars, that the subject of the election was mentioned. In a pause of the conversation Fred said, "Well, dad, what about the constituency ? "

"Bless me," said Mr. Hazzleden, "Mr. Arnitte and I have had such an interesting chat that I forgot all about business. It's a seat at Dockborough, and is now held by a Tory. But he's not a popular man, and besides, has given great offence to the Irish electors. If you can please them without offending the Whigs you're sure of a small majority. Have you, by the way, any views on Irish policy ? "

"Fred is partial to the Irish," said Arnitte, cracking a nut.

Fred could not tell why a flush, half of anger, half of shame, burned in his cheeks, for there was no spark of malice in the clear eyes which met his across the table. He answered with embarrassment, "Of course I think the Irish have been very badly used for hundreds of years, and we · owe them every reparation. Besides, the Prime Minister knows better than any one else what to do, and I'm quite ready to follow him."

Mr. Hazzleden impatiently strummed on the table, and Arnitte quietly remarked, "You have a great deal to learn in politics."

Fred was beginning to resent his friend's calm assumption of superiority—an assumption, he thought, hardly warranted by the difference of their years. He answered warmly, "I don't profess to be an experienced politician, but all my life has been passed in England, and I've thought a good deal about affairs. It seems to me, if I pledge myself to support every just measure of relief for Ireland, and to follow the Prime Minister faithfully, the Irishmen will be satisfied, and the Whigs ought not to quarrel with me."

"You really suppose," asked Arnitte, "that justice and faith count for anything in politics? My dear fellow, you are fitter to be a minor canon than a member of Parliament. Except by exalted enthusiasts, such as the Premier, these considerations are never thought of. At the present time your Irish friends want reform, partly for revenge and partly to spoil the landlords. The fact that their cause is that of justice is only an accident. The Whigs and Tories care nothing about the question for itself, but they know that while this Irish question blocks the way they are safe. All they want is to dish the democracy. The masses are puzzled and are waiting to discover which side pays best before they make up their minds." ·

"I don't believe it," said Fred. "If I did I would take to cabbage-growing rather than enter public life."

"You'll find out before your election is over," Arnitte grimly rejoined.

Mr. Hazzleden, to his son's surprise, intimated that Fred was evidently a baby in politics, and that Arnitte was right.

The latter exclaimed again, "Why, when we were at Lorton I picked up a local paper with a speech by the Tory who is going to contest the county. What did the fellow tell the agricultural labourers? Not that Irish reform was right or wrong, or good or bad for the empire, but that if it was passed Irish labourers would flock over here to all the farms, and wages would go down. I don't defend it. I say it's thoroughly contemptible. But he'll go in, and he wouldn't if he had taken any other line. My contention is that English politics is a mixed business, and that, if you are going in for it, you mustn't be too nice."

Fred eagerly replied, "He was a Tory; that's what the Tories always do. They appeal to the basest passions of the mob. But I am a Radical; I believe in the justice and honesty of the people, and the only appeals I will ever make to them shall be on grounds of justice and right."

"I admire your enthusiasm," said Arnitte, "but you'll never be member for Dockborough."

The evening was hot, and Fred, rising, threw open a window and stepped out on to a small verandah. He called to Arnitte, and the pair, lifting out their chairs, sat down to finish their cigars. Mr. Hazzleden slipped away to join Aunt Maria.

Fred was saddened. Here was a young man, with little experience, but high ideal of public life, hearing upon its threshold that the only means of entering was to fling away his ideal. The game already began to seem not worth the candle. He was in the habit of bringing all problems before the bar of reason and conscience. He imagined that other people did the same, and that in a constituency, as well as in an individual, the judgment of this tribunal must be supreme. The gospel of pocket *versus* principle always seemed to him too base to be influential, yet if Arnitte and his father were right it was the one thing he was to preach. He was half inclined to abandon all idea of Parliament. Would it not be better for him to marry Kate and settle down at Lorton? This last thought left him more perturbed than before.

Arnitte sat by, his chair tilted back against the wall, his feet on the railing of the verandah, puffing out the smoke in rings, and silently reading the troubled questionings of Fred's mind.

"You're disgusted with the whole business," he said.

Fred, half angrily, grumbled an assent.

"I'm pretty quick at understanding character," replied Arnitte, "but there are some things about you, Fred, I admit I can't make out. You aren't fickle or weak, yet you seem to keep no grip on your convictions. One moment you think you're in love, the next you think you're not. Then you're consumed with political ambition, and now you find it a mean passion. Forgive my frankness; I know our short friendship scarcely justifies it."

Manifestations of personal interest always touched Fred, and he replied, " I believe you're right, Arnitte. I haven't understood myself of late. I seem to have no roots at all."

Arnitte swung round. " Let me try and give you one. Don't fling up public life because the way to it isn't as pleasant as you hoped. Stick to your ideals all you can, and remember this : methods which the best men in your country—the Prime Minister, for instance—don't shrink from adopting, can't be

wholly bad. You're dealing with an unedu-
cated democracy and an intensely selfish
aggregation of classes. You must make some
concession to their fears and prejudices, if
you want them to give you the opportunity
of doing any good at all. If I were stand-
ing for Dockborough I would learn to
catch votes without abating a jot of my
self-respect."

Fred was consoled without being convinced. They rose and went into the house.
In the drawing-room they found Aunt Maria
with Mrs. Williamson, who had called to pay
an evening visit. Mr. Hazzleden, in his easy-
chair, his head tipped back, his elbows on the
arms, and finger-tips meeting, was meditating
on the origin of species. An open volume of
Darwin lay upon his knee. According to his
wont he had set the women chattering, and

then, tired of their talk, had gone off into a dream.

After the introductions Mrs. Williamson continued with great earnestness, "I were saying to your Haunt Maria, Mr. Fred, that this here evolution theory won't do."

"Contrary to the revealed word of God," said Aunt Maria. "Oh, fools and slow of heart to believe all that the prophets have spoken." She looked affectionately towards her brother, and Mrs. Williamson shook her head and sighed dolorously.

"Is it not written," continued Aunt Maria, "'Man was made upright, but they have sought out many inventions'? Yet, Mrs Williamson, they would have us believe that man was made on all fours, and only learned to stand upright by his own cleverness. In the pride of their stubborn free will they seek out many inventions, which do but humble them to the level of the beast that perisheth." Aunt Maria raised her eyebrows until her forehead seemed gradually to fold itself up into the roots of her hair, and she gazed at Mr. Hazzleden as though she expected him to frisk barking round the room on his hands and knees, or to squat jabbering like a monkey on the floor.

"It's an insult to us," said Mrs. Williamson, taking up the parable. "My family was most respectable people, and never 'ad no relations with hapes or any other disgustin' beasts." When Mrs. Williamson's shallow mind was stirred up her aspirates were tremendously emphatic. It was consequently a pity that, as a rule, they fell in the wrong places.

"It's all nonsense and 'ortiness of 'art, as you say, ma'm," she went on. "Besides, are we to think that the patriarchs and apostles, and even 'olier ones than them, was descended from the hugly reptiles as orgin-grinders carries about with them ?"

"That is conclusive," said Aunt Maria; "the same thought has occurred to me. Explain it away if you can, John. By your irreligious theories you would compel us to believe that the Being whom we worship was descended from the beasts. Could anything be more shockingly blasphemous ?"

"I can't explain anything," said Mr. Hazzleden; "I'm sleepy and going to bed," and with brief "good-nights" he retired. Aunt Maria folded her hands and smiled triumphantly. Fred, who, like his father, was utterly bored, would have been glad to escape, but Arnitte, with the manner and tones of deferential courtesy which were usual in his conversation with ladies, had taken up the discussion and was leading the pair of theologians through the most grotesque dilemmas. There was no suggestion of irony in his demeanour. A man of coarser fibre would have "drawn out" Aunt Maria and Mrs. Williamson for his own amusement. Fred was quite sure Arnitte had no such intention. He had the art of finding pleasure in all subjects and all persons. He had discovered two types of character new to him and was studying them with grave interest. Fred at once acquitted him of all discourtesy, but he was thankful when the discussion ended and Arnitte condescended to go to bed.

CHAPTER VIII

THE following day a deputation from the Dockborough Liberal Association waited upon Fred. It consisted of Robert Davies, Esq., merchant, the President, and Arthur Bradley, Esq., solicitor, the Hon. Secretary. They were an interesting couple. For many years past, over daily lunch in the local Reform Club, they had settled the political affairs of Dockborough. Every one distrusted them, every one abused them, yet every one appeared to believe that they were essential to the Liberal party. The Dockborough Liberals had an elaborate representative organisation, and at committee meetings fiery Radicals thundered out denunciations against the "hole-and-corner" management which was ruining the prospects of the party. There was an epithet of local significance which was frequently applied to them. They were called the chiefs of the "strawberry jam" clique. Who invented the term and how it was derived no one knew; perhaps it was adopted because of its subtle suggestion of social superfluity. At any rate, to have a banking account and pretensions to refinement were to be "strawberry jam." If Lord Dockborough, the president of the club, gave a dinner to the heads of the party, or if the newspapers reported the presence of Messrs. Davies and Bradley at a reception at the Foreign Office, or if a rich Liberal was made a Justice of the Peace, the sturdy Radicals muttered, "strawberry jam again," and felt greatly relieved by the scornful ejaculation. But Messrs. Davies and Bradley kept their places and continued their oligarchic rule. The reasons were, that they were the only men in Dockborough able and willing to pay for their political hobby, and that they were really the ablest and most experienced party tacticians in the constituency. The imputation of "strawberry jam" they bore with tranquil resignation.

A short time before their visit to Fred the pair met at the lunch table. Mr. Bradley had just returned from a business mission to London.

"Hullo!" he said; "how's things?"

"Pretty well, thank you; how are you?" replied Mr. Davies, who had a weakness for small jokes. This was their customary salutation.

"Got hold of any one yet?" inquired Mr. Bradley as he studied the bill of fare.

"No," grumbled Mr. Davies; "we've got such a beastly bad name nobody worth having will look at us. Tell you what it is, Bradley, we shall have to put you up to give Lawson a run."

Mr. Lawson was the sitting Tory member.

"Not good enough, Robert," replied Mr. Bradley. "Prophet in his own country, you know."

Mr. Davies disconsolately consumed his mutton cutlets and a half-pint of thin claret.

Presently Mr. Bradley carelessly remarked, "I saw the Whips on Friday."

"Of course you did," retorted Mr. Davies irritably. "I wish you'd drop those lawyer tricks and speak out. I knew you'd heard of some one when you came in."

Mr. Bradley was moulding a piece of bread into a large pill, his eyes were fixed on a gilt star in the decoration of the ceiling, and he seemed to hear nothing.

"One of the Midland members has recommended to them a young chap named Hazzleden who lives near Soarceter," he continued. " I knew his father years ago."

"Not a philanthropist I hope, Bradley," said Mr. Davies impressively.

Mr. Bradley winced slightly. At the last general election he had a brilliant idéa. He secured a worthy man who knew nothing about politics, but whose lavish charity made him very popular in the constituency. The worthy man recited half a dozen speeches which Mr. Bradley wrote for him, and won the election. But a month or two after he was unseated on petition. The costs were heavy, and they came out of the pockets of Messrs. Davies and Bradley.

"He's only a lad," resumed the latter, "not long from Oxford. He spoke well at the Union and took a good degree. That's about all you can say of him. The old man, who's a Tory by the way, wants to send him into the House and will pay up, which is the main point, Robert. You know as well as I do that there's precious little chance of any one turning out Lawson, and we only fight to save our credit."

"Not much left to save," Mr. Davies blandly interposed.

"True enough. But, you see, we're between two fires. I wasn't very cordially received at headquarters I can tell you, and if we don't fight we're done there. Then the Association will be turning up rough again."

"Think we can get the Association to take this young sprig?" inquired Mr. Davies.

"Oh, damn the Association," said Mr. Bradley.

"Wish I knew how," piously murmured its president.

"Look here, Robert," said his friend, "if you won't be serious I'll chuck up the whole business."

Mr. Davies raised his hands in affected consternation.

Taking no notice of the grimace Mr. Bradley proceeded, "You can lead them by the nose if you like. If I were you I'd quietly spread it about that the Council is thinking of selecting him, and, by the way, you might get a puff in the papers—member of old family, brilliant young man, distinguished university career, strong Liberal convictions, and all that. We can easily make them think that they've discovered him themselves, and then they'll jump at him."

Mr. Davies smiled sweetly and stroked his curly brown beard.

"But for goodness' sake say nothing about the money. Those fellows take a delight that's positively devilish in bleeding us."

Mr. Davies smiled again, and remarking, "You're a nice man, Bradley," sauntered away, devouring with apparent relish the pointed end of a wooden toothpick.

It was a foible of Mr. Bradley to coach his friend, who, to use an expressive colloquialism often applied to him in Dockborough, "knew his way about" as well as most men. Within a week the members of the Liberal Executive were running everywhere dropping

mysterious hints that an absolutely invincible
candidate was shortly to be produced, and
the principal local paper one morning "understood that negotiations were in progress with
Mr. Frederick Hazzleden of Barkleigh, one
of the rising hopes of the Liberal party, a
gentleman of high social position, brilliant
university career, and unusual oratorical and
political attainments, with the view of in-
ducing him to contest the seat." Whereupon
Mr. Bradley addressed an indignant letter to
the editor, intended for publication, inquiring
on what authority a statement was made
which was, to say the least of it, premature.
This was the final stroke. The "General
Council" of the Association assembled next
evening, and Mr. Davies warmly protested
that the members, in unofficially considering
the question of a candidate, and communicat-

ing with the newspapers, had not treated their officers with becoming courtesy. A chorus of deprecation and denial followed, and then, without a single dissentient, Mr. Frederick Hazzleden was invited at an early date to address the Association. Messrs. Davies and Bradley, who always paid their own expenses on such expeditions, were deputed to visit Barkleigh, and make the necessary representations to Mr. Frederick Hazzleden.

A certain sect of Dissenters has the custom, when any one wishes to join the denomination, of despatching to the "candidate," as the aspirant for admission is called, two members of the church, selected for the occasion, and known as "messengers." These messengers examine the "candidate" in the articles of faith and belief,—especially those articles which constitute the peculiar distinction of the denomination,—and subsequently make a formal report to the church in meeting assembled, as to the candidate's fitness for communion with the saints.   One may well wonder how the numerical strength of the sect is maintained in spite of an ordeal so severe.   Fancy a trembling young housemaid called upon to demonstrate her Scriptural information and doctrinal soundness, beneath the cold eyes of a brace of deacons in the solemn privacy of the back-kitchen!   How any one can manifest creditable theological attainments under such conditions is a marvel.

Fred felt a good deal like the young housemaid when he entered his father's little library and discovered two gentlemen drinking port wine with Mr. Hazzleden.   One was a big loud-voiced man; the other a slight, short individual of subservient tones and gestures, and a face which reminded one slightly of the Christ's head in the Leonardo fresco. The big man, Mr. Bradley, was smiling on Mr. Hazzleden, but as Fred walked in he turned his smile upon the son. It was a remarkable smile, and people in Dockborough said it was worth £3000 a year to its owner. It produced under and at the side of the eyes, a series of transverse wrinkles, and it drew the mouth up at the corners, showing the side teeth as an angry dog does, while concealing the front ones. It had no meaning which any human being had ever been able to discover. It was not Mr. Bradley's natural laugh, which was simple and jolly enough. He only used it in business, and then the person upon whom it was turned began to feel a sort of hypnotic helplessness.

Mr. Bradley directed upon Fred his business smile and shook his hand. "Glad to see you, Mr. Hazzleden. And *how* are things?"

It was a peculiarity of the honorary secretary of the Dockborough Liberal Association that he rarely waited for an answer to his questions. Until you got accustomed to it the habit was annoying. Now, he was paralysing Fred's faculties with his smile, and furtively measuring the future candidate from head to foot, little concerned about his opinions on the state of things.

"How d'y'do?" said Mr. Davies; "hope you're all right and hope you'll be right honourable some day." The president laughed softly and rubbed his hands.

Fred remembered the first time he stood before an awful apparition in cap and gown

after he went to Rugby, how very small he
felt. Until the present moment he had
never felt so small again. His first thought
was that his visitors were drunk, his second
that he himself had gone mad. Mr. Hazzleden, senior, who understood the situation
much better than his son, at last came to
the rescue.

"Sit down, Fred," he said, "and take a
glass of wine."

Fred mechanically obeyed.

Mr. Bradley relaxed his smile, and remarked, "Now we can get to business."

"We've heard, Mr. Fred," he said, "that
you wish to fight a seat this election,
and we've come to ask you to address the
Dockborough Liberal Association. They told
us great things of you at headquarters, and
the constituency is just the place for a

clever young man who wants to make a beginning."

Mr. Bradley began to smile again, and Fred turned hastily to his companion. "The present member is a Tory?" he asked.

"Well, you see," said Mr. Davies, "we were rather unfortunate. We fought last time with a capital candidate—a very good man, very good indeed. But there was great indiscretion somewhere, wasn't there, Bradley? Lawson petitioned and the case went against us."

"What was your majority?" inquired Fred.

"Two hundred and forty-seven," said Mr. Bradley, who had a head for figures. "Small, perhaps, but sufficient."

"Some of your people were scheduled, don't you call it?" carelessly remarked

Fred. "Doesn't that mean that they can't vote this time?"

The deputation opened their eyes. This was more than they had bargained for. They expected to meet a green college lad who knew no more about scheduling than about sheep-stealing. As a matter of fact Fred had had a long conversation with Arnitte that morning, who, with the help of Dodd's *Parliamentary Companion*, had posted him in the recent political history of Dockborough.

"Ahem," ejaculated Mr. Bradley, "we did unfortunately lose a few voters. But Lawson is very unpopular—a member who wins by petition always is. Then there's a considerable Irish population which will move heaven and earth to get you in. Of course we can't promise you a safe thing, but if you work you'll stand a firstrate chance."

" And about expenses ? "

"Seven fifty," murmured Mr. Davies.

" Well," said Fred, " I think I understand
the situation. A young man ought to fight
a doubtful seat for a beginning, and if my
father consents, and the Association will have
me, I'll stand."

Mr. Davies and Mr. Bradley rose and
shook him by the hand, assuring him that his
sentiments did him honour, and that the
Government would be grateful to them for
introducing such a candidate to public life.

Mr. Hazzleden expressed his approval of
the arrangement, and invited the deputation
to remain to luncheon.

At table, aided by Arnitte, Fred cross-
questioned the deputation as to the state of
parties and opinions in Dockborough.

" We're a little mixed, it is true," said Mr.

Bradley, who had just begun his second pint of champagne, and was growing confidential. "First, there's the Whigs. Davies has always been able to manage them before, and I hope will do so again, but we must confess they're jibbing. They're chiefly the shipping people—men who have made money; some have been made knights and even baronets, and they're very respectable. Oh yes, damned respectable."

Aunt Maria dropped her knife and fork with a great clatter and rolled her eyes wildly, but Mr. Bradley was a man upon whom delicate hints were wasted. He was absorbed in Pommery and politics, and continued serenely :

"Then there's the Irish—a rum lot, who all went Tory last time. They made things very lively, I can tell you. They called

Davies 'buckshot spouter' on his own platform."

"And they dubbed our friend here 'the
devil's attorney,'" interrupted Mr. Davies.

"They're penitent now, and will vote
straight to the last man. You can't get both
the Whigs and the Irish, I'm afraid, though, of
course, the Whigs will find it hard to desert a
country gentleman. But our main trust must
be in the great mass of the people. The
heart of the people nearly always goes right,
doesn't it, Robert?"

"Yes," repeated Mr. Davies, solemnly fill-
ing his glass as though for a toast, "the great
heart of the people nearly always goes right;
and the great vote of the people," he added,
sotto voce, "nearly always goes wrong."

"Now you know the difficulty of the
situation," resumed Mr. Bradley. "The

seat is Liberal without a doubt, and if the fight went on strict party lines Lawson would lose by at least a thousand. But the Dock-borough Liberals, especially the leaders, have peculiar views, and you'll have to humour them. For instance, there's old Sir Alexander Bligh, who's withdrawn from the Association because the *Daily Gazette* argued that men with more than a million were a public nuisance, and ought to be suppressed. Little Alec, who'll come into the money when the old man goes, has put up for the Tory Club."

"Little Alec's a fool," said Mr. Davies with quiet decision.

"Damned fool," said Mr. Bradley fiercely.

Aunt Maria had retired, so the expletive didn't matter.

"Would it not be best," asked Fred, "for

the candidate to go his **own** way, saying what he thinks and believes, without trying to humour anybody?"

"Best for Lawson, decidedly," said Mr. Davies.

"But," continued Fred, "even if it were dignified or honest to trim, it would be useless. For instance, if I win over this man Bligh, I shall lose five hundred of the people in doing it."

"My dear boy," replied Mr. Bradley as he pushed the bottle across the table, "you'll learn a great many surprising things in the next few weeks. Old Bligh is a popular man. He pays his clerks as much as £250 a year, and his work-people get fair wages and constant employment. Of course they've helped to make the baronet's two and a half millions. Now, if you proposed to do something which would take away some of his money-bags, and distribute the contents among his employés, Bligh would raise Old Harry to get you defeated. He'd tell his working men that you were a communist, socialist, and perhaps an atheist, and they'd all go against you. If you get Bligh on your platform, and talk of the commercial glory of Dockborough, and say a judicious word for existing institutions, Bligh will call you a safe and enlightened Liberal, and the voters will shout themselves hoarse for you. Of course I don't mean to imply that the great heart of the people isn't sound——"

"He only means," said Mr. Davies, "that the great head of the people is devilish soft."

"Don't be flippant, Robert," retorted Mr. Bradley. "I want our candidate to have a good idea of the constituency. It's a

great help to a man to understand the
people he's fighting among. By the way,"
he continued, "you're not married, are
you?"

Fred answered that he was not.

"Pity," said Mr. Bradley.

"But he's going to be," exclaimed Mr.
Hazzleden.

"Ah," was the languid rejoinder. Outside politics Mr. Bradley's sympathies were
dull.

"What advantage would it be to me to
be married?" asked Fred. "I mean," he
added, reddening, "as far as my ~~election
prospects are concerned.~~"

"Well, you see," Mr. Bradley explained, "nothing goes down with a public
meeting like a young wife, pretty and well
dressed. And then in canvassing she's in-

valuable. All she has to do is to smile and look nice, and the effect is enormous. Ten years ago young Douglas, who's now gone to the Upper House, poor fellow, carried the seat, and his wife did it all."

" How ? " inquired Fred.

" How ? Why, by sitting next him on the platform, and looking as pretty as paint—that's all. On the polling-day, during the dinner hour, we made her drive to the booth through the labouring quarter with a very dirty working-man in the carriage beside her. It was a fine touch, and served us splendidly. Davies made her do it, and she never forgave him. She vowed that she didn't feel clean for a fortnight."

" Well, I fear," said Fred with a little sigh, " that I shall have to do without such pleasant assistance."

"Couldn't Kate go with her mother to Dockborough?" said Mr. Hazzleden. "My niece," he explained, "the lady to whom my son is engaged to be married."

"Not nearly so good as a wife," said Mr. Bradley. "People aren't sentimental and make fun of engaged couples. Spooniness is no good in politics. You couldn't get married at once, I suppose now?—archbishop's license, private ceremony for family reasons, and that sort of thing."

Fred feared not.

In the end it was decided that if Mrs. Wynnston was willing, she and Kate should visit Dockborough during the election and work for Fred.

After the deputation had gone Fred felt sick at heart. He rushed out to avoid Arnitte, whose cool sarcasms would have driven him mad. He found a shady spot at the top of the orchard, and flung himself down on the grass and lighted his pipe. This was his introduction to public life; this was the avenue to the honourable career which his imagination had pictured. Why! the dirt of the few paces he had gone would stick to him for ever. What would he be when he had waded on to the House of Commons? Then he was ill at ease about the invitation of Kate to the election. He had been more tranquil since his departure from Lorton. He had begun to consider his marriage as a distant event which must be regarded as a matter of course. He had even learned to think with warm affection of Kate. But he was not eager to see her again so soon; he had had sufficient experience of the region of storms for a while. Musing thus

Fred let his pipe go out and at last fell asleep.

The deputation were driven to Barkleigh station in Mr. Hazzleden's carriage.

On the way Mr. Bradley remarked, " Good Pommery that ! "

" Seventy-four, I think," said Mr. Davies.

There was a pause, and at length Mr. Bradley spoke again. " Young man isn't altogether a fool. He'll make a good fight when we've licked him into shape."

" Poor devil ! " said Mr. Davies, and the pair relapsed into silence.

END OF VOL. I

Printed by R. & R. CLARK, *Edinburgh.*

Lightning Source UK Ltd.
Milton Keynes UK
UKHW020701060119
334942UK00006B/562/P